Over 100 Great Novels of Erotic Domination

If you like one you will probably like the rest

New Titles Every Month

All titles in print are now available from:

www.adultbookshops.com

If you want to be on our confidential mailing list for our Readers' Club
Magazine (with extracts from past and forthcoming titles) write to:

SILVER MOON READER SERVICES

Shadowline Publishing Ltd
No 2 Granary House
Ropery Road
Gainsborough
DN21 2NS
United Kingdom

telephone: 01427 611697
Fax: 01427 611776

NEW AUTHORS WELCOME

Please send submissions to
Silver Moon Books
PO Box 5663
Nottingham
NG3 6PJ

Silver Moon is an imprint of Shadowline Publishing Ltd
First published 2006 Silver Moon Books
ISBN 1-903687-84-5
© 2006 Richard Garwood

Painful Performances

By

Richard Garwood

All characters in this book are fictitious, and any resemblance to real persons, living or dead, is purely coincidental.

This is fiction - In real life always practise safe sex!

Painful Performances

"I'm going to die," Sarah thought to herself, "and perhaps this is the way to go."

She stood on a low platform looking out at the people in front of her. The hall was lit only by the large candles which stood either side of her. She could smell the acrid smoke they gave off as well as the perfumed sweat of the spectators. They were dressed in exotic robes, copied from some arcane religion, and each held an emblem of status amongst the ranks of the companions. There were some twenty of the devotees and they eyed her speculatively as a drum beat steadily in the background.

Sarah wondered what they made of her. She knew she was imprisoned in a wooden frame with her hands and feet tied to the four corners. She was quite naked. Her blonde hair had been tied up behind her head, and the preparation for sacrifice had included the removal of all her body hair. She could feel a slight coolness between her thighs and looking between her breasts could see that her vulva was quite bare of any defence from view. She tried to wriggle her body into a slightly more comfortable position, but the effect of her movement was to do no more than part her labia and reveal the pink tip of her clitoris. She felt a flush of embarrassment steal up her neck. Why should she be embarrassed? She hadn't asked to be displayed. Not that she didn't enjoy the appraising stares of those in front of her. She didn't know just what was to happen to her next, but thought that it would be painful and frightening. She was fearful, and yet she revelled in being the centre of the viewers' attention. She tried to move her arms but found that her breasts bobbed slightly as a result and her ribs seemed to become more visible through the thin covering of flesh.

There was a cry from the devotees and two of them came forward and stepped on to the platform. Each of them took a breast and kissed the nipple until it stood out from the areola. As if by some signal they clipped a dangling silver figurine to each nipple. The pain of the closing clip was little enough to worry about, but Sarah was surprised that her already full, but solid and out thrusting breasts were beginning to become turgid.and heavy.

The pair left the platform and another couple arrived. They caressed her body for two or three minutes and then one slipped a hand down between her thighs and began to massage her vulva. Sarah felt herself become moist and then a pressure at her vulva as something was inserted into her vagina. So much had she concentrated on this event that she had blocked out of her consciousness the entry to the portal between her buttocks of something very similar. Suddenly Sarah felt very full.

The penetrating couple was replaced by two more members. They grasped the dildos which had been inserted into Sarah and moved them about. The smaller man pressed hard on the dildo in her rectum which very nearly met the one in her vagina. The taller of the two operated at the front and had large hands. Knuckles grazed Sarah's clitoris and she felt a tide rising within her. As it became more insistent the couple stood to one side and a further member mounted the platform and placed a blindfold over Sarah's eyes. The other member of the pair placed a forefinger on her bottom lip whilst sharply pressing the thumb of the other hand into her navel. Sarah's surprise made her open her mouth to cry out but at once another dildo was pushed between her lips and used as a gag.

Sarah heard the latest of her tormentors leave the platform. Suddenly she felt the wooden framework to which she was tied begin to revolve whilst remaining vertical. She realised that she would have her back to the viewers, and then she lost all idea of which way she was facing. The drum beat went on monotonously. She felt another presence on the platform. Something dry and slightly rough was placed over her shoulder and then drawn away. She felt fingers at her waist as a leather belt was inexorably tightened round her. Someone stood behind her and moved a ratchet a couple of clicks to tighten the belt even further. Sarah was glad she carried no surplus weight.

There was silence for a minute and then the drum beat started again, this time very slowly. On the second beat Sarah felt a sudden burning sensation across her back and at the fourth another which crossed over the first. She realised that she was being whipped, and by two people. Her buttocks received the next strikes and she tried to shake in her bonds. The effect was to drive the dildos further into her body. The whip snaked again across her bottom from the other side and the tip curled round the outside of her thigh.

There was a pause and she felt the frame move again. Presumably two more tormentors had arrived.

They soon made their presence felt by blows to her side just below her breasts. Sarah was becoming breathless from the pain and the dildo in her mouth. She jerked her head back and then down and suddenly her mouth was empty and she heard the thump of the dildo as it hit the edge of the platform and rolled away. To her amazement she heard what sounded like a murmur of approval.

The frame moved again and Sarah pressed with all her might against the dildos still in her. She felt the one between her buttocks begin to shift and then to slide out giving her an uneasy feeling of emptiness. Try as she could she was unable to dislodge the thing in her vagina and each pressure she exerted made her feel closer to an orgasm. She felt the ratchet being tightened again and wondered how small her waist had become and how her ribs and hips must jut out beyond the constricting belt. There was little time for such thoughts however as a hand reached round from behind her and with its thumb pressed against her clitoris pressed a button on the pulsating vibrator sunk deep in her belly. Sarah had a vision of herself totally visible and vulnerable and now being forced into an orgasm which she knew would be all consuming. She began to gasp and threw her head back with her mouth open. Lips were at once pressed against hers and a probing tongue entered her mouth. Sarah's shoulder and thigh muscles clenched and she felt the boiling orgasm hit her belly. As soon as she started on the irreversible route the mouth and the dildo were removed and she hung racked with waves of passion as the juice poured from her in what seemed an unstoppable stream.

"I'm going to die," she thought, "and this is the way to go."

But neither was true.

As she reached almost the end of her climax she felt the whip catch against her thigh. She knew she was being beaten, but she had gone past pain into that amazing euphoric state that comes with the takeover of endorphins. Someone ripped off her nipple ornaments, whilst her waist was suddenly released from its constraint. Another hand removed her blindfold.

"It's all over now," she thought, but that wasn't true either.

She turned her head in time to see a tall figure on her right raise a whip and before she had time to blink the tip had stung her left breast with a devastatingly well aimed blow.

She screamed and at once a sharp blow from the other side caught her right breast.

Sarah had hardly caught her breath when the whips struck her waist and one tip buried itself in her navel. She howled, but the pain was far from unbearable. There was a pause, and Sarah looked down at the assembled group. Unexpectedly she suddenly felt as if something red hot had been thrust against her vulva, and realised that the whip had found her swollen clitoris. She waited for its pair to repeat the agony but it didn't come. Instead nimble hands were untying her legs which fell together with her toes just touching the platform.

Her legs felt wobbly, and her feet were too little in contact with the platform to give support to her body. A tormentor came towards her with some leaves in a gloved hand. Suddenly Sarah felt the fearful prickle of thistles on her bottom and then two slashes across her breasts took away her breath. There was a pause and she felt a thin cord being tied round her waist. From this was hung a small bunch of leaves and the whipping began again. It took Sarah several seconds to realise that these leaves were stinging nettles and that the pain was excruciating. She tried to move her legs back so that the leaves hung forward only to receive a startling strike across her buttocks with the same plant.

Sarah danced in agony, her breasts jiggling to every movement of her legs and body. She tried twisting only to find more excruciating blows from bunches of leaves. The blows continued but she was beyond feeling them and fell into shock, finally hanging motionless from the frame with her head drawn back and her breathing stertorous.

She was hardly aware of the hands taking her down from the frame or being laid on a bed covered with a white sheet. Suddenly, there were four sets of hands massaging every part of her body with slightly acrid leaves. The burning pain which had overcome her senses started to leave her.

Dock leaves, she thought, the only real palliative for stinging nettle pains.

Sarah sighed and lay back finding the touch of the hands agreeable. She closed her eyes and wished that the hand that was treating her belly would see to her pussy. No sooner was the thought in her mind than it was turned to action and her legs were parted and the soothing leaves were rubbed, none too gently, between her thighs. She wanted to pull her deliverer towards her and express her thanks for the kindness she was being shown, but she knew all too well that such a thing was forbidden. She was the toy of the devotees and must submit to their wishes in all things without initiating anything for herself.

Someone was holding her head up and presenting a cup to her lips. Sarah opened her mouth and swallowed what tasted like a draught of spiced punch. She could feel it going down her throat and warming her stomach. She turned her head to see who had given her this very agreeable drink when the world started to go out of focus. Her last thought was to do with the effects of alcohol on an empty stomach.

*

Sarah woke in a room without windows and with no discernible door. She was lying in a comfortable bed. Gingerly, she felt round her. There was no one else in the bed, despite it being at least king size. Her hand encountered a bedside cabinet. There seemed to be a wire hanging from it. She followed the wire with her fingers and came upon a switch. She clicked the button and very slowly a dim light suffused the room. A quick look round showed that it was without other furniture and that there was an archway to her left which led to what might be a bathroom. Sarah realised what it was that had awoken her and carefully stepped out of the bed. She was delighted to find a room with a sink, loo, bidet, shower and bath and a big pile of thick white towels, together with deliciously scented soap and shower gel as well as body spray. Judging by the rather elaborate razor and shaving foam beside the sink, the room was normally occupied by a man-or was it?

Sarah made use of the loo and the bidet and then decided to have a shower. The water gushed over her and gurgled into the waste pipe. Steam rose around her and the scent filled her nostrils. She took a deep breath, turned off the shower, stepped out of the cubicle and proceeded to dry herself with one of the towels. She felt she wanted to comb or brush her hair, but there seemed to be nothing with which to do so. She made her way back into the bedroom to find the bedside cabinet drawer open and a beautiful tortoiseshell comb and hairbrush visible. She plied both with considerable vigour until her long blonde hair shone and hung in a straight curtain round her head. She looked for something with which to tie it back, but could find nothing.

She had no idea what the time was. She knew that something to eat would be pleasant, but she had no idea how long she had slept. She wandered back to the bathroom and inspected herself in a wide two metre high mirror. Each breast had a small mark on it, the legacy of the whip. There were other marks but they were quite inconspicuous and could pass for a small mole or birthmark. Sarah found them unusual, because her skin, like her life up to the recent past had been protected and perfect.

Sarah wrapped herself in a large bath towel and sat on the bed. Her mind was less concerned with the future than her past. At least that was certain and she could do nothing about either the future or the past. She sat quietly staring into the corner of the room as images of her life swam before her eyes.

She recalled a happy, safe and generally agreeable childhood. Life had seemed very secure and happy. There were relatively few rules, and in any case she was not a rebellious or awkward child, so that she didn't mind doing whatever it was she was asked to do. After a year at the secondary school she started her periods and she began to grow a fine fleece between her thighs and under her arms. She became popular with the boys at school, and had a couple of staunch girl friends with whom she could discuss almost anything.

Sarah began to blossom at about thirteen. She noticed that her jeans no longer fitted her bottom and that her school blouse was far too tight across her chest. Her mother took her to the school outfitters and they came away with bras, close fitting panties and a variety of clothing suitable for school, some of which was embarrassingly designed for her to grow into.

Altogether hers had been an ordinary, quite innocent childhood and she had grown to her mother's height of 165 cms She had never acquired the customary coating of puppy fat but her body had developed wide hips, a narrow waist and beautiful breasts. Her hair had darkened from ash to honey blonde and her blue eyes were fringed by naturally dark and long eyelashes and sharply defined eyebrows. Sarah was beautiful, but had no idea of the effect she had on other people.

She had gone off to university at the age of eighteen and had done well on her chosen sociology programme. For some reason connected with the subject of her studies and her self valuation, she had remained a virgin, at least technically.

Then she had fallen in love. She sighed at the memory. Nick was as dark as she was fair. He was ten centimetres taller than Sarah and strongly built with powerful hands and long, muscular arms. There was something about him that attracted her at once. He was one of those all too rare men who carefully listen to what a woman has to say, consider it and reply thoughtfully. He didn't like readers of celebrity magazines, but he did enjoy a conversation on almost any subject, except football and sports generally. Everyone has a particular weak point, and Nick's was a blanket disregard for professional sportspeople, and particularly footballers, who he regarded as overpaid, cosseted yobs, with neither manners nor brains between them. Surprisingly, despite his avowed lack of interest, he could name twenty or thirty instances, with names, to back up his prejudices.

Nick introduced Sarah to the outdoor life, and in the long, warm summer after graduating, he took her on a walking holiday, carrying what little they needed on their backs and heading for such wilderness as still exists. She recalled how wonderful it was to wake up in the fresh air and bathe in a nearby stream. Breakfast was prepared in the grass and the unbreakable plastic plates cleaned where they had bathed. Sarah had discovered the delights of skin contact and then the pleasures provided by a couple of questing fingers whilst firm dry lips kissed hers and then sought her nipples. On the very first occasion that this had happened she had failed to have an orgasm and Nick had not penetrated her. An hour or so later she had put her arms round Nick's neck and implored him to do it again. They were standing in a clearing in a wood and Nick removed her T-shirt and jeans and ran his hands all over her for what seemed a very long time before adeptly finding her clitoris and bending his head to suck her nipples. She continued to clasp her arms round his neck and, as far as she could, pressed herself against him, only to come into contact with his rigid penis. She remembered giving a gasp as she felt it against her hip and slipped her hand down to feel it, realising that it was too thick for her to get all but her longest finger and her thumb round and too long to encompass in one hand. It seemed to have a life of its own and made her vibrator seem a very ineffective implement. Sarah enjoyed foreplay, but on this occasion it was all too brief before she had a gushing orgasm. She cried out in delight and suddenly realised that Nick had slipped an arm under her buttocks and had easily lifted her off the ground and was letting her slide slowly down his belly until she felt the tip of his penis pressing against her vulva. She opened her legs and Nick lowered her until his shaft penetrated her. Still her feet were not touching the ground and she steadied herself by winding her arms round his neck. At last she was fully penetrated and her toes were touching the fallen leaves. Nick had seized a buttock in each hand and had raised and lowered her against himself. Sarah had thought her earlier orgasm was all she could manage, but as his thumb struck between her buttocks she gave herself over to another mind numbing and seemingly unstoppable orgasm whilst she could feel the throbbing pulse of Nick's ejaculation filling her. He took control of both their bodies and lowered both of them to their knees whilst he still faced her. Very slowly he withdrew from her and held her head steady as her eyes became misty. Without thinking she told him that he was wonderful and it was wonderful and she leaned her head on his shoulder. The stream came in very useful again half an hour later.

Those were halcyon days, but summer gently turned into autumn and the outdoor life became less agreeable and there was work to do and money to be earned. They had returned to the city. Nick had at once been taken on by his uncle who ran a clothing manufacturing business and retail outlets. Sarah had sought some temporary employment and had drifted into a factory manufacturing sweets. She became the quality controller on the production line, picking out misshapes from the literally endless lines of chocolate coated sweetmeats flowing past her for eight hours at a time. She became adept at the job which required nothing but concentration on little moving shapes whilst she had all the time she needed to think about Nick and the future and her next job and what she had learned during the last three years. She began to develop her plans for the future. Whatever else, they were sure to include Nick, who had opened an entirely new world of love and passionate sex to her. She could feel herself being drawn deeper and deeper into his life and needing to do whatever was necessary to keep him and their life together.

One evening Nick came home carrying a dress bag which seemed to have something quite voluminous in it. Sarah was woman enough to be very interested in clothes and inquisitive enough to want to know what Nick had brought home. He had seemed slightly less than forthcoming until she pressed him and he unzipped the bag and started to lay the contents out on their bed. She remembered how amazed she had been. Sarah had never seen what Nick described as SM clothing before and was most intrigued by the leather straps, the studs and the spikes and the carefully placed gaps which would reveal what most clothing was designed to cover. She had quizzed Nick about it. He had been off hand and told her that his uncle's designer was working on a new range and that they were looking for someone to model it. Sarah didn't see herself as a model and particularly of these remarkable clothes and she had said so. Nick had told her to leave them alone because someone else would have to wear them and they needed to look brand new.

Nick went off to his Karate class and Sarah sat for a while in front of the TV, but didn't bother to switch it on. Eventually she got up and went into the bedroom. Nick would never know, she thought, and she slipped out of her T shirt and bra and attempted to put on the top part of the garment. Anything that is mostly straps takes some organising, but she eventually got it the right way round and pulled it down over her body. There were numerous adjustable buckles, but she found she didn't need to use them. As she had expected, a good deal of her breasts and the whole of her nipples were visible regardless of how the straps were adjusted.

She had discovered two straps which hung down at the back and which appeared to be intended to be connected to buckles at about waist height. She was quick to pull off her jeans and thong and pull the straps forward round her hips. This wasn't going to work so she crossed them over and tried again. That didn't do anything either. It occurred to her that they were intended to be brought between the legs either side of her pussy. She tried it and the fit was perfect. The wardrobe door had a full length mirror inside it and she walked round the bed and opened the door. She had been amazed by what she saw. She seemed to be transformed by the fetish gear into a darkly wanton creature. She had wondered if Nick would like it, but as she stood admiring herself she suddenly became aware of Nick standing in the doorway.

"I didn't think you could avoid interfering, even when I told you not to."

"Oh, I'm sorry, Nick, I didn't mean..."

"How can I trust you when I ask you not to do something and you immediately do it. I wouldn't do such a thing to you." Despite the rather priggish sentiment, Sarah could see that he was furious. She stood with her hands in front of her, feeling dejected and wondering how she could put things right.

"I really won't ever do anything again that you tell me not to."

"That's not good enough. How can I get some girl to model these when you've already worn them?"

"I am truly sorry, Nick."

"I ought to make sure you are." Suddenly Sarah had felt a shiver of anticipation.

"Yes, please, so long as it makes things right between us."

Nick shuffled the remaining things on the bed and extracted what looked like a small leather paddle about 45cm long. He held what appeared to be the handle in his right hand and brought the flat end down on his big open hand. The thwack had made Sarah jump.

"How do you fancy that on your bottom?" Nick asked.

Sarah swallowed hard. She couldn't believe that she felt it was what she wanted more than anything in the world. She dropped her head and whispered that he must do what pleased him. Sarah had never been smacked or seriously punished in her life, come to that she had very seldom been told off, and here she was, inviting a punishment of unknown pain.

Nick sat on the bedroom chair. "Come here," he

commanded and she came to his side. "Lie across my lap."

Sarah had little idea how to accomplish this but she soon found that the straps enabled Nick to move her about until her feet just touched the carpet on one side, whilst her hands held her up on the other with her hair fallen forward over her face. Nick was presented with the wonderful cloven moon of her bottom. He touched her gently with the paddle as if measuring the distance and then brought it down sharply across her buttocks. Sarah emitted a little cry, possibly more of surprise than pain. Nick looked at her bottom with the pink flush from the first blow showing the outline of the paddle. He could see the thin fleece of her vulva and the slot of her labia protruding slightly between her thighs. He brought down the paddle again, harder, and Sarah shuddered. He struck her a third time and was surprised to notice a fine dew at the gates of her sex.

A fourth and a fifth blow followed and Sarah began to moan, though she made no attempt to get away from him.

Six, seven and eight were delivered hard and fast and Sarah started to shake.

"Have you learned your lesson?" Nick demanded.

"Oh, no. I need to be punished properly," Sarah replied.

Nick, faced with the beautiful, trembling and acquiescent body of his lover, had worked out that there was more to this than setting matters right between them. Here was a side of Sarah's character that he had not encountered before. He started a steady tattoo of blows on the tops of her thighs and her buttocks.

Sarah's squirming appeared to have little to do with avoiding the blows. She realised that she was wet between her legs and that she was close to orgasm. Nick paused in his beating and pushed his fingers into Sarah's vagina whilst pressing a knuckle against her clitoris. At once Sarah let out a great cry, half of pain and submission, half of exquisite delight. Juice ran from her and on to Nick's jeans whilst she felt a positive hail of biting cuts from the paddle. At last Sarah seemed to subside and Nick threw down the paddle and pulled Sarah up into a sitting position on his lap. She put her arms round his neck, touched his face with her breasts and whispered that it had been wonderful and told him how much she loved him.

Nick had carefully removed the basque with straps and had pulled back the bedclothes and deposited Sarah into it, drawing the duvet up just below her breasts. She reached out for him and he slipped out of his clothes and into her, to their mutual satisfaction.

These reminiscences were interrupted by the sound of a panel in the wall being slipped back. A voice asked if she was all right, to which she replied that she was hungry.

"Very well, have you any particular desires?"

Sarah thought she would leave the choice to the unknown visitor and said so. The panel closed and Sarah continued to sit on the edge of the bed reviewing what had transpired in her life.

There was one great advantage with Nick, she thought, though that wasn't true, there were many. At least it was possible to talk to him about almost anything, come to that, anything at all.

The following morning she had told Nick that this had been an experience which had changed her life.

Even if that were not yet true, it had certainly changed her view of herself. "I loved being in your power, I loved it when you beat me. I wish you could punish me and hurt me every day."

"Not every day. There has to be a variety in being alive to make different things enjoyable. Otherwise it's like having an unrelieved diet of chocolate."

"But you don't know how I felt."

"You forget I had quite a bit of evidence." Nick grinned wryly. "Besides, I knew you couldn't resist wearing this kit. I also knew that you would look stunning in it. I promised Uncle George that I would get him the most beautiful model in the business to be in the catalogue. So you're hired."

"Hang on! If you knew I'd do it, then why were you so angry with me?"

"How else did I get to punish you?"

"But you couldn't have known I would like it."

"Well, I had an idea you might, but in any case I knew I would, and I needed an excuse to try it out on you."

"You scheming sod!"

"So it's bad to have a few deviant ideas?"

"Oh, no. It was wonderful..."

Sarah had been concerned about the photo sessions, but was introduced to the photographer who was much more interested in Nick than he was in Sarah. He moved her about for best angles and his touch was light and respectful. He accidentally touched her right nipple and as she stiffened he apologised at once. It was not his thing, he told her, and she could believe it.

The first prints arrived two days later and Nick brought them home to show her.

"Didn't I tell you that you'd be fantastic? Just look at these."

Sarah saw herself revealed for the first time. These were not pictures like the seaside snaps in a bikini. In those it was evident that she had a flawless figure. In these there was dark passion and she looked the embodiment of eroticism.

"These will make uncle's fortune, and could be a start on ours."

Nick had plans for Sarah and himself, but what they were he wasn't then prepared to divulge.

*

A meal arrived for the imprisoned Sarah which was beautifully cooked chicken with a Moroccan sauce and fluffy Basmati rice. The dessert was a crème caramel of delicious lightness topped with crunchy sugar. The coffee was fresh and smooth rather than the usual acrid dregs forced on the British. She decided that the chef was a sound person and wondered if this had been lunch or dinner. The dishes were removed and in their stead came a pile of magazines ranging from the drivel in cheap celebrity mags to serious treatments of difficult issues in sociological journals. A thoughtful choice, and she tucked herself up on the bed to start with the rubbish. She'd finished two of these when the panel slid open and she was told that it was time for her exercise. Another, much larger panel opened and she went out into a carpeted corridor. She followed her guide and was shown into a room about six metres square which contained many varieties of exercise machine. A formidable woman in a white coat handed her a thong and indicated that she should put it on.

"First thing is we have to photograph you so that we can see if there are any changes over the period of your training. Stand on that spot there with your hands on your hips, and get rid of that towel."

Sarah did as she was told and the formidable lady produced a digital camera from her pocket and proceeded to take pictures of Sarah, front back and sides.

"Now I want you to jump up and grasp those rings. Right, good. Now open your legs and point your feet."

Sarah did as she was told and many pictures of her almost naked body were stored on the memory card. She was glad she had combed her hair.

"You can call me Vanessa," Sarah was told, "though this won't be a social occasion."

It turned out to be very hard work. Sarah had been to a gym quite a few times, but gentle exercise and a careful attention to what she was eating, to say nothing of some remarkably helpful genes, had given her a beautiful, if not particularly toned body. She was told that there would be an hour and a half session every morning and afternoon, and that if she wasn't making progress after ten days there would be an evening session as well, unless it got in the way of her other duties.

"What other duties?"

"I am training you to be a suitable member of the club. Now get on with it."

The getting on consisted of running on the treadmill and then moving to the weights which she used lying down, sitting up, and standing. It wasn't that they were particularly heavy, but that there were so many timed repetitions. She tried her best at the whole of the regime including press ups, skipping, walking, running, stepping up and down with alternate feet onto a box, bending forwards and back and sideways and attempting quite difficult tasks with the hanging rings. For the first time in her life Sarah was very pleased that her breasts were firm, but she was the only person who wished that they might have been a bit smaller. The session ended with five minutes in a vertical tanning enclosure and a twenty minute sauna. Vanessa came into the sauna with her, put a folded towel on the bench, unbuttoned her white coat and sat next to Sarah quite naked, displaying a figure of heroic proportions with muscles visible at every point. Her skin was golden brown and her dark hair curled down her neck. As with Sarah, she was devoid of body hair.

"This ought to take away any possible aches you might have. If you do ache tomorrow we can order you a massage."

Sarah did ache and she had her massage provided for her by a Chinese man who hardly spoke to her. There followed another session of training, and in the afternoon another one. At teatime she was allowed out with Vanessa in the beautiful gardens of the house and wandered among the flowers and bushes breathing in the soft, warm air.

"I'm surprised you didn't want to be out here before this," Vanessa said. Sarah sensed a trap.

"I've learned that it was not what I want that matters, but what I'm given and what is required of me that is important."

"Quite right."

*

In the evenings Sarah was tired. Three, or sometimes more than four hours of rigorous physical activity each day may have strengthened her physically, but she found that the soft bed was most welcome. Her bedclothes and towels were changed every day. Her room and the bathroom were spotless. She thought they might be claustrophobic, but laughed at the idea, because within them she had everything she required and considerable comfort. A life which has a regular routine is easiest to live. There are no unwelcome surprises, though Sarah knew that sooner or later there would be.

She considered her position in relation to what any animal might do when threatened. She could fight. But who would she fight, and was there any point in fighting if there was no possible chance of winning? Then there was flight. Could she run away from Vanessa when they were in the garden? Where could she run to? What could she do if she was, as was generally the case, virtually naked? Then there was acceptance. She thought she might well survive and she might just as well make the best of whatever situation she had got herself into.

Despite all the physical activity and her tiredness in the evening she wanted Nick to be with her and hold her in his arms. She drifted off into a reverie of the events after the catalogue photographs had been taken.

Nick had been delighted with the pictures and so had his uncle. Nick told her that his uncle was going to pay Sarah for her work. "You shouldn't be doing that awful job any more. I think a lot of opportunities are about to open up."

"Oh, yes. Such as what?"

"Well, it depends on you."

"Go on."

"Tell me how you felt about having your photos taken practically naked, in fact better than naked."

"I really didn't mind."

"What about the audience? There was the lighting man and his assistant and the props man to say nothing of the photographer."

"He was no threat and the rest of them didn't bother me at all. To be honest I liked the admiration."

"That's what I wanted to hear. There's a chance for you to appear in a very high class entertainment. Good money, appreciative audience and things you might like."

Sarah looked doubtful. "Is it sleazy?"

"I don't do sleazy and in any case the greater the fee the less sleazy it is."

"I don't think I understand."

"Well, it's like this... No, the easiest thing is for you to see what happens and then consider if you'd like to be involved. You'll need to wear that fetching lace dress and I'll pass you off as Uncle George's daughter."

"Why can't I go as myself?"

"You'll see."

Nick had made a few phone calls and the following evening they drove out in a hired Mercedes to a very smart house in substantial grounds. They were admitted through the electric gates to a valet parking arrangement which meant they had only a few steps to go to the front door. As it swung open Sarah was bathed in a warm light. Nick looked at her with delight. The dark red lace dress was almost backless and the front was cut sufficiently low to reveal the full curve of her breasts. The lace clung to her body down to her hips so that it was just possible to distinguish her nipples and her navel. Below her hips there was a split at the front which showed her thighs when she walked and only the briefest covering of her crotch. It was a dress to be very careful in, especially as Nick had insisted that any form of underwear would spoil it. Sarah had reluctantly agreed and had quickly learned to get out of the car with her knees pressed together.

They were ushered into a large room which was the epitome of opulence. The people were dressed and made up beautifully. Apart from some dress jewellery in her hair, which she was wearing up in a neat chignon, Sarah was devoid of jewels, whilst all around her women positively glittered with diamonds, rubies and emeralds.

There was an area devoted to dancing on a raised, sprung platform. Around it were tables and chairs, some occupied by couples and groups who were engaged in serious drinking or delicate eating, or both. Nick suggested that they might have a dance. The music was quiet and slow, so that knowledge of the steps seemed less important than ensuring the closest possible contact with the partner. Sarah saw several people who she thought she vaguely recognised, but she was more interested in Nick than in the strangers. She folded her wrists and hands round his neck and looked up into his face. He was conscious of the pressure of her body all the way down his and began to have those stirrings which the very close proximity of a beautiful woman can create for a man. He was glad his dinner jacket was long enough to allow him to indulge his delight without it being obvious to anyone but Sarah.

"Nice music," she breathed in his ear, "Very, very seductive"

Nick laughed and moved his hand downwards on her back, pressing her towards him.

The music played on, but they had eyes only for one another. Suddenly, a very powerful spotlight picked them out from the other dancers. A voice came from a public address system.

"Universally agreed to be the prettiest couple on the dance floor. We do hope we shall see a lot more of you soon. Take a bow!"

There was a round of applause. Nick bowed and Sarah attempted a deep curtsey forgetting the dangerous dress. The spotlight seemed to penetrate every part of the lace and there were some appreciative noises from the audience as she recovered herself. She turned to Nick and kissed him.

They walked off the dance floor and found a table where a bottle of champagne was chilling in an ice bucket. A waiter deftly opened it ensuring that neither of them received the cork or the champagne spray.

"Well, I don't seem to remember anything like that at college balls," Sarah said.

"No, but then have you any idea how sensational you look?"

"Do tell me."

"You look utterly innocent and at the same time quite ready for any entertainment which might be going."

"You've got the second part right. Where's the entertainment?"

Nick looked at his watch. "It looks to me as if we have twenty minutes to go. Shall I fetch you something from the buffet?"

Sarah knew all too well that this meant that Nick was hungry and she nodded.

By the time that they had consumed Nick's choice from the buffet and Sarah had visited the Ladies room to fix her make up, the music had stopped and the tables were swiftly cleared of everything but bottles and glasses. Sarah looked around her. Everything spoke of money. She had occasionally visited the sort of houses that she suspected the guests came from and on the whole she preferred something less excessive, even downright shabby, provided that Nick was there.

The lights dimmed and there was a murmur of expectation. A ripple of applause greeted the entry of three dancers who floated across the floor. Each was dressed in an almost transparent shirt, open at the front but secured by a belt at the waist. As they leaped and pirouetted the audience was treated to tantalising glimpses of breasts, buttocks and neatly executed Brazilians. The man with the two women was as dark as Nick, whilst the women were blonde and auburn respectively. The tempo of their dance increased and the man tried to catch first one and then the other of the women. So far his success, as they ducked and twisted, was reduced to pulling off the blonde's belt. Sarah realised that her nipples and areola had been made up in dark green to contrast with the pale skin. In a matter of moments the redhead had lost her belt and then her shirt, but she managed to twist away from the man and escape. Frustrated by his pursuit of the auburn woman he turned his attention to the blonde, but whilst she was smaller than her companion, she was also even quicker. Breasts bounced, bodies twisted and then the two women seemed to act in concert, each seizing a wrist and pulling the man's arms behind his back. The blonde had snatched away the man's belt and secured his wrists with it. His shirt fell open to reveal a well toned body with a singular erection. The women held onto his arms with one hand whilst the other was involved with what was protruding from his groin.

The redhead started to stroke him whilst the blonde cupped his balls in her hand. He tried to evade their attentions and pulled his hips backward. A hard grasp by the blonde quietened him. He shook and shivered but the outcome was inevitable and the sharply spurting jism was adeptly caught in a discarded shirt by the redhead. The lights switched off to some not very enthusiastic applause.

"We could do that at home a lot better," said Sarah, slightly louder than she had intended. There was a snort from the next table and a whispered conversation.

The spot lights came on again to illuminate a girl and a man. She was wearing a white dress and he was conventionally dressed in shirt and jeans. There was music, much like that which had played when Nick and Sarah had occupied the dance floor. The girl put her arms round the man's neck and looked into his eyes. They clung together moving slowly and sensuously to the rhythm. After a minute or two the man pulled at the back of his partner's dress and a section of thin cloth from the neck to the bottom of her spine floated away. This was obviously going to be a strip tease and Sarah waited to see how they would manage it and whether the girl's figure was as delicious as little hints made her think it was. The next to go was a strip of cloth below the neck which left the breasts almost wholly exposed, but still pressed against her partner. There was more dancing and then the dress skirt was bisected at the front so that it appeared that she was uncovered from ankle to navel. The music became a bit faster and they drew away from each other whilst holding each others' wrists. It was time to see that the remains of the dress were an exaggeration of Sarah's, at least she hoped it was an exaggeration and she dropped her hands into her lap encountering, to her surprise the bare skin of her crotch.

Sarah wriggled in her seat to ensure that she was decent. She wondered why she bothered, given the nature of the entertainment, but then, perhaps the audience wasn't supposed to join in. The couple were embracing again and the man lifted his partner, apparently effortlessly. By some means that Sarah failed to spot the man had lost his jeans and standing sideways to the audience he lowered his partner on to his erection and having achieved all the penetration that was possible they danced again for a few moments whilst the man went through the appearances, at least, of screwing his partner. As the spotlight went out there was some more, not very enthusiastic applause.

Nick leaned across to Sarah. "I wonder where they got the idea for that dress? It reminded me of something."

Sarah looked down at herself and realised that her recent squirming had pulled down her décolleté until her left nipple was visible at the upper hem of her dress..

"Beautiful," said Nick, "and deserving of a wider audience."

The lights dimmed until there was almost total blackout and then the spotlight picked out the figure of a girl dressed in what looked like numerous varying length strips of white cotton fabric which covered her from the shoulders to her ankles. Her arms were held rigidly above her head and her feet seemed to barely touch the floor. At this point Sarah realised that the girl was hanging from a hook above her head and was very slowly turning from right to left. So intrigued had Sarah been by the girl that she had failed to notice the figure of a man dressed entirely in black and wearing what appeared to be a black mask. There was no apparent movement from the man until he slowly raised his right hand and revealed he was holding a long tapering plaited leather whip.

"Surely he's not going to..." Sarah whispered to Nick.
"Wait and see."

The man flicked the whip forwards and the tip caught at one of the strips and tore it from the girl's shoulder. She uttered a grunt as she felt the whip touch her. As she turned the man struck again and tore off three more strips, two at the back and one at the front. Each strike was accompanied by a small explosive grunt from the girl. Another strike ripped off a strip and revealed a breast, another tore off a further strip at the back and showed a gleaming buttock. The audience became intent on seeing what would happen next. Sarah glanced across at the next table to see a woman frigging herself whilst staring with her lips parted at the tableau. In the time Sarah had looked away another strip had gone from the girl's back and another from between her breasts revealing a narrow band of white skin from neck to crotch.

The blows became slower as the number of strips diminished. The girl's back was almost completely bare and only three strips remained at the front. The whip snaked out with what Sarah realised was increased power and the girl gave a little cry as two strips on the front of her body were ripped away. It was a small matter for the expert handler of the whip to tear away the remaining strips and leave the girl hanging naked and exposed before the audience. There was a round of appreciative applause, but the spotlight was not extinguished.

Sarah wondered what was to follow, but she had not long to wait. The man moved back thirty or forty centimetres and suddenly the whip had come alive in his hand and shot across the intervening space and snaked across the girl's left breast. She uttered a high pitched gasp and seemed to jump up in response to the pain. As she turned he struck a blow across her back and was rewarded by a jerk of her body and a sharp cry. The next cut fell across her belly with the tip of the whip on her hip. She moved her legs apart to ease her pain and was immediately rewarded by a flicking cut between her thighs. She let out her breath in a sudden explosion and Sarah noticed how prominent her ribs were and how her breasts stood firmly over them.

The girl had no time to recover from this traitorous cut when the whip struck her across the back with the tip encircling her side and ending against her breast. She shook herself and gave a low moan. As she turned she received another blow to the belly and then a flick to the breast. She started to shake in her bonds, but still the inexorable turning proceeded and still the whip stung her body, one across her buttocks which made her lift her leg in defence and as she did she received another hit between her thighs. She started to dance in her agony and Sarah noticed that the inside of her thighs shone.

With no sense of mercy or kindness the whip was plied across the naked body and then again between the thighs from behind, and as she turned again, from in front. At that the girl threw back her head and howled and received another blow to her cunt and she shook and cried out and arched her pelvis. As another cut fell across her vulva she screamed and juice started to pour from her as her screams turned into a long, rough edged, animal howl from a mixture of pain and sexual release.

The shaking and the stream of juice became less violent and she hung from the hook with her body stretched out defencelessly and her head thrown back in total abandon. The roar of applause made Sarah realise that she had been pulling at herself between her thighs and was very close to her own orgasm. The woman at the next table had been quicker and more open than she had.

The spotlight dimmed, the two figures left the floor and Sarah turned to Nick.

"That was amazing! She loved it, pain and all! What a gorgeous girl and that man was a real expert with the whip! I'd really like to meet them."

Nick was on his feet at that and disappeared amongst the tables. He was soon back.

"They have a dressing room up the back stairs and we are welcome to visit them." Nick grabbed a couple of bottles of champagne and twisted his fingers round the stems of several glasses. A footman joined them and preceded them up the stairs and along the corridor to their left. He came to a door and knocked. There was a muffled invitation to come in, the door was thrown open and there stood the two performers wrapped in each other's arms and very little else.

"Oh, should we..." began Sarah.

"Come in and sit down. We both need a bit of relief after a display and there's no better way that I can think of."

"Nor me," said Sarah. "I thought you were both wonderful."

"Thank you," replied the man shrugging himself into a dressing gown. "I'm Ivan and this is Tania."

"We're Nick and Sarah," Nick said and poured long glasses of champagne.

"I gather you want to talk to us," Tania said.

"Oh yes," Sarah replied. "Does it hurt as much as it appears to?"

Tania opened her dressing gown to show the weals across her skin and the hard dots of brown where the tip of the whip had cut into her.

"It hurts, but you'll notice the technique. It would be easier for me to appear naked right from the start and for Ivan to thrash me so that everyone could see just what was going on. After all they come here to get off on a pretty girl being whipped and then coming. What we do is prepare me for what is to come. The cloth strips are there so that the whip is relatively gentle for a start. You might have noticed that the blows became slower but heavier towards the end of the stripping. By the time we are half way through the punishment the hormones that whipping releases have won out and I can hardly feel the agony. When I start to dance I am doing it for myself. I just love displaying my body and I love the admiration of the audience, though most of all I enjoy Ivan whipping me. I wish he could be naked too, but that would detract from my nakedness and I know he couldn't resist fucking me there and then."

"Oh, yes, that's true," said Ivan. "We did a gig once in a big country house and the owner suggested that I should be painted red and made up to look like the devil. I wore a tiny thong which matched the paint. Halfway through the punishment it broke free and I had to continue the performance with a raging erection. At the end I caught Tania up in my arms and had her right there on stage. It was some of the best sex we'd ever had and it brought the house down alright!"

"Why didn't you do that tonight?" Sarah asked.

"We're trying to work out a new routine, something a bit more stimulating."

"More stimulating!" Sarah cried, "I very nearly came myself."

"Pity you didn't," Ivan replied, most of the audience did.

"How did you start off in the business? I think I might be embarrassed to show myself naked, though I think I'd like it."

"We had a three week holiday in St Tropez," Tania told her, "and spent the days on the beach at Ramatuelle, after that it was fairly easy. Of course, they weren't paying to see me on the beach, but they certainly looked."

"In any case the audience is there only to admire us and get what pleasure they can."

"Do you suppose they all go home and sort each other out?"

"I suspect so, but you have to be the right sort of person for this sort of display. Besides, despite what you might think, we have to rehearse and I've spent a good deal of time perfecting my technique with the whip."

"Did you do it on your own, or can you get lessons?"

Ivan smiled a wolfish grin. "Why don't you come to our studio? I'm sure Tania wouldn't mind Nick having a little practice, provided that we can also have you as a pupil."

Sarah looked at Nick, who was well into his fourth glass of champagne.

"Why not. When would suit you? "

So it was all arranged and three days later Sarah and Nick had turned up at a green door in a wall in a back street in Chiswick. Sarah thumbed the intercom and announced their presence. There was the sound of several heavy bolts being drawn and the door slowly swung open. A powerful light came on over their heads and they saw a set of stairs in front of them leading up to the first floor. As they moved across the hallway the front door snapped back to the closed position and the bolts were returned to their sockets. Only then did the door at the top of the stairs open and Ivan appeared in jeans and a T-shirt. Sarah was suddenly taken aback at how threatening he appeared. They sat down and were being given coffee when Tania arrived dressed in a beautiful, delicately flowered kimono. The conversation dealt with the weather and the parlous state of sport and then it was Ivan's turn to ask questions.

"Why do you want to learn the mysteries of our art?"

Sarah, much to her chagrin, blushed. "Well, a little while ago Nick found me doing something which he had told me not to do. We both thought I ought to be punished and he used a leather paddle on my bottom. I suddenly found myself enjoying it, but I wanted more, and more variety and rather more in the way of ritual attached to it, and then we saw you."

"And are you thinking of going public?"

Sarah and Nick both answered together, but their replies were not the same. Nick looked hard at Sarah.

"You know perfectly well you'd get off on displaying yourself and being admired."

"Yes, but, well, we haven't discussed it."

"There's not much point until you know if you're suited to it," Ivan observed.

Tania put her head on one side and smiled at Sarah. "You seem to have all the necessary qualifications apart from experience, and we can help out there."

"Look," said Nick, "we're taking up your time and benefiting from your expertise. We ought to come to a business arrangement before we go any further."

"Ah! A gentleman!" Ivan replied. "If you're going to be professionals then we will want to be your managers and take ten per cent of the gross."

"That's a brilliant idea, but I'm a bit worried about going into competition with you. We aren't ever likely to be as skilled or as good as you are."

"There's no question of competition," Tania replied. "We get three times as much work as we can hope to deal with. You'll appreciate that this is not exactly a five day a week job. I like to have four days between gigs so that the weals will have vanished or at least I can mask them with make up, and in any case they don't hurt and I'm ready for more."

"Are there any permanent marks?"

"No, we never cut the skin, though we have simulated it on occasion."

"How...."

"That's a not very abstruse trade secret which we'll let you into in due course."

Ivan stood up. "Come along you two, we'll go into the studio and see what the raw material looks like."

The studio was a room about ten metres by six with a double door at the far end which looked as if it might lead into a store, a shower cubicle in the corner and a thick rubber mat over its floor. The windows were high up in the wall and the room appeared not to be overlooked.

"This used to be part of a warehouse. All the walls and floor were built twenty-seven inches thick and there is no chance of any noise penetrating here or getting out. The windows are triple glazed. Now, please remove your clothes, hang them over there and have a shower."

With only the slightest of resentments at the implications of the request they stripped and showered and dried themselves on warm white towels.

They stood, a slightly uncomfortable pair, in front of the shower.

"You're naked, we're not. You're going to have to learn that being naked among the clothed will be a very usual state of affairs, and the first thing to do is to stand up straight and smile. Now Nick, just go over there to Tania and I'll deal with Sarah."

Sarah wondered just what 'dealing with' meant, and

wondered if it would be painful or embarrassing. Both Tania and Ivan had produced note pads and pencils. Ivan looked hard at Sarah and made a few notes on the pad.

"Open your mouth, please." Sarah did what she was told and Ivan momentarily peered inside. "Lift your arms," was followed by "stand with your legs apart, and now on tip toe." She was required to turn her back on him and to have her breasts gently squeezed and her vulva pressed with two of Ivan's large fingers. She bent over and Ivan stood back with his eyes fixed on the cleft below her buttocks. Sarah had slender legs that didn't touch all the way up. He slid his hand between them and seemed to be pleased with what he found. He lifted her hair and replaced it carefully, finally paying a good deal of attention to her knees and her feet.

Meanwhile Tania was examining Nick in much the same clinical way. Nick was probably twice the size of Tania, but he felt like a small, naughty boy as her eyes never left his body. She ran a hand over his muscular belly and applied the same sort of attention to his buttocks. After a searching examination of his limbs, feet and torso she came to his side and touched his testicles. He felt her hand tighten, but not enough to give real pain, "Nice solid balls in a tight scrotum," she murmured, and transferred her attention to his penis. "Do you find it difficult to have an erection in public?"

"Well, I've never....."

"Not even with one or two strangers?" She smiled and gathered his flaccid penis in her hand and flipped it up against his belly. "Or would you prefer Sarah to give you an edge?" He realised that this was a rhetorical question as her hand moved up and down the shaft of his penis and he felt it growing in thickness and length. He soon realised that he was fully turgid.

"Are you afraid to come in public?" she quietly asked and found her hand become sticky with the first glistenings of his orgasm. She quickly removed her hand and left him standing with his erect cock jutting out in front of him. Sarah caught sight of it and made a face at him.

They were called together and Ivan started on his analysis of Sarah.

"Beautiful face, excellent teeth, lovely hair, stunning figure, nice feet. But, you will have to have a Brazilian and then use some cosmetics on your vulva. You've got good projection when you bend over and you keep your clitoris in its pouch. Can you produce it for us, please?"

"What, now?"

"Of course."

Sarah reached between her legs and parted her labia. She rubbed a couple of fingers on her clitoris and it stood up and shone in the midst of her vulva.

"Bend over, please. Ah, good, an excellent view, should it be needed. Will it go away?"

Sarah gently kneaded her labia over the clitoris, but it wasn't anxious to disappear.

"You have a beautiful body, but it is more feminine than toned, and striking it will be more painful than if you had a layer of muscle underneath the skin. I can see your ribs and the arch above your belly, but for this job they might well be rather more prominent. I suggest four visits a week to the gym, but avoid running as you might do those wonderful legs no good at all. Upper body work only."

Tania smiled at Nick, whose erection had not subsided. "Everything is fine here, but you have body hair. You'll have to get rid of all of it. I can recommend a good salon. I suggest you both go to it and both visit the gym together just to keep you in good shape.

Now, let's start on a little tuition." She opened a box. "Here is a variety of whips and tawses. The bull whip, which Ivan uses on me, needs a lot of practice. Most of these are easy to use though not as spectacular. Your aim is to engage in the maximum of ritual and to provide your audience with the maximum of spectacle. Come with me a moment."

They went to the double doors at the end of the room and Tania pointed to a dress maker's dummy. "Bring that out and I'll show you what to do."

Nick's lesson proceeded in an unexpected direction. Meanwhile, Sarah was learning from Ivan. She wondered just what she had got herself into and was seriously concerned at Ivan's rather chilling attitude to her. Somehow, she felt that he hardly viewed her as a human being, but as a target.

"There are all sorts of poses you can adopt, which we will explore later. There is also the matter of your movements. Do not make sudden or unexpected movements. Your partner may fail in his aim and you might be hurt more than you would care for. I have no idea what your reaction to the display of your naked body or the application of a whip might be, so perhaps we should find out."

Ivan reached up to the wall and pulled down a metal bar which was hinged to the wall and once it was at right angles it locked into position. A rope ran over a pulley and there was what appeared to be a pair of handcuffs hanging from the end. He paid out the rope until it came to about Sarah's waist level.

"Put the cuffs on."

Sarah trembled at his order. Her nakedness and her fear of Ivan combined to make her feel very vulnerable. She thought of her delight in Nick's masterly treatment of her, but Ivan was a degree of magnitude different from Nick. He was obviously a professional dominant and being big and forbidding in appearance reinforced her fear of him and his intentions. She reluctantly obeyed his instruction. Ivan checked to see that she had got the cuffs fitted correctly and then began to pull the rope over the pulley. Sarah's arms rose until she began to stretch and her heels left the floor. Ivan took his camera from his pocket and started to take more pictures, instructing her to turn as he did so. Sarah was happy to exhibit what she knew to be her perfect body, but had been chilled by Ivan's touch.

"Good. Now I am going to whip you and we will see how you take to it. If you want to wimp out of it, say so, but remember that will be the end of our arrangement." He fixed a blood pressure and pulse rate monitor to her right arm.and stood back to see the general effect. If he approved of what he saw he gave no indication other than to flick out the whip with practised ease to catch Sarah across the buttocks. She winced and thrust out her pelvis.

She was halfway through another turn when Ivan unleashed a blow to her belly. She gave a quick huff of breath and drew air into her lungs. As she turned Ivan caught her across the waist and then across the back. These were light blows but the pain was intense. Sarah's pulse rate had increased substantially and her breathing had become deeper with her breasts rising and falling on her chest. Ivan was beginning to count. The fifth cut took her just below the breasts and brought a grunt from Sarah. Six and he caught the tip of the whip across her right nipple. Her cry was slight but penetrating. Ivan criss-crossed her back and bottom with three quick flicks as she turned and Sarah shook herself to ease the pain. The tenth, eleventh and twelfth blows all landed on her belly and across the top of her thighs, Sarah moved her legs against one another and pulled her head back between her arms to look at the ceiling. A harder cut left a weal on her bottom and another crossed her back, two more fell across her breasts, Sarah became aware that Tania and Nick had broken off their lesson and were standing to one side of Ivan watching what was in progress. She wished she had never let herself be treated like this.

Tania whispered to Nick, "Hope she can hold out a bit longer, she looks like she's about to go into phase two."

Ivan struck Sarah repeatedly across the hips, thighs and back, she uttered cries and moans which disturbed Nick, but he kept his concerns to himself. He wasn't in charge here.

"What's phase two?"

"The hormones begin to kick in. It starts with dopamine. They suppress the pain and give you a wonderful high. The only problem is they can become addictive."

Ivan was well on with the thirtieth of his count and about the sixth of his harder blows. Sarah had thrown her head back and stood with her legs parted and her body arched with her crotch protruding. She no longer moved but presented a picture of abandonment to her agony. Ivan drew back the whip mercilessly and caught Sarah a few centimetres below her navel. Sarah strained back even further and opened her legs wider. Ivan flicked the whip up between her thighs and caught Sarah a cutting blow to her vulva. Her howl was unearthly and prolonged and accompanied by a slow writhing of her body. Ivan turned to Nick and handed him the whip.

"But I've never..."

"Then this is your opportunity to try."

"But what if...?"

"Do it, now."

Nick swung the whip from right to left in an arc from floor level to across Sarah's belly. There was speed and weight in the blow and Sarah cried out, but tightened the forward arc of her body. Nick pulled the whip forward over his shoulder and caught Sarah across the breasts. She emitted a harsh grunt mixed with a howl and Nick moved to her front.

Tania drew his attention to Sarah's inner thighs. Nick was amazed, but knew he shouldn't have been. He shortened his grip on the whip and brought the plaited leather up between Sarah's knees. The tip flew out behind her buttocks but the thicker part of the plait caught Sarah between her labia, opening them to show her inner lips. Sarah cried out again and started to move her knees up and down alternately. She realised that the pain had begun to have a quite different quality and that things were happening to her body over which she seemed to have no control. Despite the vile pain of the repeated cuts, she was conscious of a sensation in her vagina spreading across her belly presaging the beginning of an orgasm.

Nick caught her again, but this time with the tip of the whip and cut into her swollen clitoris. There was a moment of silence and then Sarah began to tramp with her legs, writhe from side to side and forwards and backwards and howl like some animal caught in a bitter trap. Juices began to run down her thighs and her mouth was a circle of agony and ecstasy.

Nick stood back and Tania seized the whip and sharply cut Sarah's cunt three times. The howl became a scream and the jerking showed every rib and muscle in Sarah's upper body. Very slowly the jerking and writhing slowed down and the scream became no more than a low moan. Tania turned to Nick.

"Now give her every inch of cock you've got."

Ivan had lowered Sarah's limp body to the padded floor and had removed her cuffs. Nick crouched over her and leaned forward to kiss her. His erection had not failed him and he lowered himself between Sarah's legs and guided himself into her hot and moist depths. He thrust to the fullest depth of his body and ground himself against her clitoris. Sarah's eyes opened and she looked at him as if he was completely out of focus and then raised her arms to his neck and drew him down towards her mouth. For a little while Nick remained motionless, but he could feel the intermittent grip of Sarah's pelvic muscles. He drew back and plunged into her again and again until her cries of overwhelming delight alerted him to her imminent orgasm and he thrust at her with all the considerable strength he could muster and spent his jism deep into her. After a few moments he rolled over on to his side taking Sarah with him and cradled her head against his arm. He was almost unconscious of Tania providing a cushion for his head and Ivan covering them both with a light, warm blanket.

After about half an hour Sarah stopped her involuntary shivering, awoke and stretched against Nick who stroked her back with his free arm, marvelling at the network of welts inscribed on the soft flesh.

*

Over big mugs of hot sweet tea, they stared rather bemusedly at Tania and Ivan.

"You're wondering what we think, well we reckon that there are all sorts of other stuff you could do. You two really put on some show for a pair of beginners! You showed ruthlessness and the way to respond to ruthlessness. Now the important point is how you feel about it."

Sarah looked at Nick and he took his cue to be honest.

"I thought Sarah looked amazing under the whip! And I was really jealous of Ivan and desperate to join in. When I did I loved how the whip felt in my hand and the noise it made when it hit her. It didn't seem to matter that I was hurting her because she was getting off on the pain so much."

"How about you, Sarah?"

"I haven't come to terms with it all, yet," she replied. "But I do know it'll always be one of the biggest highs of my life. I was scared shitless before we began, but I liked being hauled up until I was helpless. I loved being naked in front of other people but I hadn't got a clue about how much the whip was going to hurt! It really, really stung and I nearly cried off but there was something about the pain I couldn't resist.

"Then things began to change and I wanted to offer myself unconditionally and my head began to buzz and I wanted more and then more and I didn't care how agonising it was. I wanted an excuse to give myself to your eyes and to enjoy whatever it was that was happening to me. It hurt all the time but the hurt became different, more a stimulus; a heat in my pussy and I sensed a trickle of juice on my thigh and I knew that if you accepted my offer and cut me right on my pussy I'd come almost at once, and I did and it was utterly amazing!

"I think I might have passed out for a moment because the next thing I knew was Nick crouching above me and then you had every last bit of your cock right up inside me."

"Do you think you could ever do it again?"

"Oh yes, please, and for longer, and even more dramatic, if that's possible. I want to be seen. I want to show people my pain and my agony and my ecstasy. I want to bathe in their stares and know I'm making them want to come too. Suddenly, I'm an exhibitionist."

"And what else are you?"

"I suppose I must be a masochist."

"And will you do what you are told to do?"

"Yes, of course."

"And that makes you?"

"I don't know."

"How about if I describe you as a submissive?"

"Oh, but I'm not!"

"Just about being stripped naked, disabled and whipped until you orgasm and pass out?"

"Well, I suppose." Sarah grinned sheepishly.

"In this job you have to know yourself completely. There are always boundaries to what is possible, but you will find that each experience drives those boundaries a bit further out. Now you, Nick. You are important in all this but it is not your skill that people will come to see. They might admire your body, but it is what you do to Sarah that counts. You demonstrated an ability to provide her with excruciating pain. Now what you have to do is learn that it doesn't matter what Sarah thinks she likes or doesn't, unless it contributes a further element to the show. She is the victim and the slave and must endure the pain. You'll come up with ideas of your own. You will need to ensure that you have forced her agreement to them. If you choose to go down this path it'll change you both."

Nick and Sarah made their way home thinking of what had happened to them and how they could best deal with the change.

Over the next ten days Nick and Sarah visited Ivan and Tania three times. After each visit, Nick was exceptionally careful and massaged Sarah with curative oils so that the weals and marks very quickly faded. They had tried a number of scenarios and Sarah had had an idea about making herself a garment which would fulfil the same role as the one she had seen Tania wearing that first night of their acquaintance. She had picked a beaded door curtain out of a skip, washed it carefully and had begun to attach each vertical row of beads to a collar closed by Velcro. The collar could be removed with one tug, but each line of beads was attached to it by a separate Velcro anchor which any sort of pull would leave piled on the floor at her feet.

They had both been to the salon which Tania had recommended and had come away feeling quite different about their bodies. Everything about them was now much more visible and whilst Sarah looked more vulnerable, Nick appeared more macho and rampant. They felt the unfamiliar areas of skin and at once became interested. The aroused Nick had split Sarah's labia with his fingers to find a clitoris pulsating beneath his fingers. She had grasped his naked penis to find that it felt longer, but rather surprisingly, narrower. Standing with her back to Nick she had revelled in his fingers and quickly gasped and cried out as she had the first of several climaxes. She had held on to his penis so tightly that he couldn't have come if he had wanted to. Nick had cupped her breasts in his hand and teased out even further the turgid nipples which became sticky to the touch, whilst his other hand worked again on her wonderfully lubricated vagina. After her fourth orgasm Sarah's knees began to buckle and Nick pressed her forward over the back of a low sofa which gave him a wonderful view of her slightly parted labia between the tops of her thighs. At that he pressed himself into her and lost himself in a rip tide of orgasm and spurting jism.

At their Thursday visit Tania asked if they were free on Saturday evening.

"We think it's time for you to perform for our friends. We have a discreet little club which meets here and we entertain, and sometimes a member will join in. Sometimes two or three. On Saturday we think you should be the main attraction. I'm sorry to say that these are friends so you won't get paid, but it'll be useful experience for you and we'll relay the feedback to you. Don't forget this is a specialised audience with a lot of experience of what we have to offer so don't be surprised if they're critical. Now, we need to rehearse."

And rehearse they did. Sarah produced her almost complete dress from her bag and tried it on in front of the full length mirror. She was slightly concerned that the lines of beads parted either side of each of her breasts, but Tania appeared to think that this was an added advantage.

Nick was dressed in a black leotard which emphasised rather than hid the bulge at his crotch. He was worried in case Ivan and Tania would precede them in the show, but Tania assured him that they were not going to perform as they had a gig the following day. However, they had secured the services of two girls who would be a warm up act for Nick and Sarah.

Ivan timed their act and then introduced some more business so that the whole act lasted more than forty minutes. He wrote down a series of sections and the approximate time that each would take and told them to learn it and practice any bits they were unsure of at home. Tania handed them a number of props and bits of equipment that they were to return on Saturday.

Over the next thirty-six hours it was Nick who became increasingly nervous and Sarah who was serene and positively looking forward to the show. Nick's 'What ifs' were countered by Sarah's response that it really didn't matter if it didn't go exactly according to plan, since Ivan and Tania were the only ones who knew what they had in mind and in any case she was there to be stripped naked, shown off, hurt and have at least one blistering climax. Nick would get his reward later. She made him put on his leotard and she put on her new dress.

"Now have a good look at me, Nick. Don't you think I'll make a wonderful sacrifice to your brutality?"

Sarah looked hard at Nick's crotch and was very impressed at the growth in the bulge and then the clearly delineated erect penis.

She thought back to how the woman on the next table had nearly blown her head off trying to suppress her scream of climax at Tania and Ivan's show. Well Nick was going to blow the girls' minds and she determined she was going to blow the guys'.

They arrived at 7 p.m. and were admitted as usual. A fair number of chairs had been set out in two concentric semi circles. Apart from Ivan and Tania the only other people present were two exquisite Japanese girls with their black hair tied up close to their necks. On the floor in front of the chairs was a large tarpaulin draped over something that looked the size of a large paddling pool.

"When shall we get changed?" Nick asked.

"There will be an interval with drinks after the warm up act. This will give us time to clear the floor and bring on your requirements and during that time you can nip into the store room and change. No one will bother you."

People started to arrive, most of them casually dressed in jeans and jumpers. Ivan had turned the central heating up so that the jumpers were quickly discarded. The guests were given a drink and stood about chatting easily to other guests. Nick gained the impression that they all knew one another well. Most of the guests seemed to be in their late thirties and older, and despite the informal atmosphere Nick detected the same aura of confident money as he had at their first encounter with Ivan and Tania. Two women engaged Nick in conversation but without making any reference to what he was there for. One of them stood remarkably close to him and he felt the touch of a large firm breast as she accidentally brushed against him. Sarah had attracted women and, unsurprisingly, men, who were talking to her, but hardly listening to her replies. Two of them were trying to get into the best position to look down the front of her low cut blouse which she found a bit of a joke given what they would shortly see.

At ten minutes to eight there was a sudden hush in the conversation and the door opened to admit an elderly man, just below average height, with a cloak fastened at his neck and a short white beard and moustache. Everyone bowed and he bowed in return. After this formality things went back to normal and Ivan and Tania engaged the distinguished visitor in conversation. At three minutes to eight Tania and Ivan started to usher the guests to their seats. Nick and Sarah found themselves at the end of the front row.

The main lights in the room were dimmed and Ivan and Tania removed the tarpaulin. Nick was pleased that he had been right. This was an oversized paddling pool about four metres in diameter. A sidelight glowed over the pool and the two Japanese girls arrived. They were dressed in knee length white jackets. They turned to one another and bowed deeply.

Ivan spoke, "This, ladies and gentlemen, is an

example of Sumo wrestling such as you will not see anywhere else. Please welcome Flower and Petal"

The girls took off their jackets and folded them neatly. Tania removed them to a vacant chair, and stood at the side of the pool which Nick took to be about the size of a Sumo wrestling ring. The girls were naked apart from a tiny thong which hardly did the job it was allegedly intended for. They bowed to the audience and to each other and stepped into the pool which had inflated sides about fifty centimetres high. There was a quick feint and then the two bodies came sharply together with a slap of flesh on flesh. Each of the girls grasped the other round the waist and they strained against each other until Petal gave a swift twitch and they both fell to the floor. Except it wasn't floor. In the bottom of the pool was about five centimetres of liquid, dark brown mud. Nick leaned forward to get a better view. Flower was on her side whilst Petal was trying to get a lock on her with her legs. Flower was beginning to be covered in mud whilst Petal was still dry from the waist up, but not for long. Flower reached up to Petal and grasped a beautiful little breast in her muddy hand. Petal leaned forward and was immediately turned on her back. Flower instantly kneeled over Petal, but Petal shifted her hips and threw Petal off, leaping to her feet as she did so.

Flower jumped up and circled Petal who turned to meet her. Petal stepped forward and made a grab for Flower's waist, but Flower twisted away. In doing so Petal had taken hold of Flower's thong which turned out to be remarkably strong, and she was able to quickly draw Flower backwards towards her. As the bodies collided Petal let go of the thong and slipped both arms round Flower seizing a breast in each hand. Despite the sticky mud Flower was apparently unable to release herself from Petal's grip so she reached round behind her and tried to use Petal's thong as a lever. Petal made an attempt to cover her modesty, obscured as it largely was by mud. Flower at once twisted out of Petal's grasp and reaching down pulled Petal's knees from under her causing them both to collapse in the slime. Petal was face up and Flower was on top of her looking down. She tried to get her knees on Petal's arms, but slipped off. Petal grabbed the first thing she could get a purchase on which proved to be Flower's thong. Flower tried to defend herself and sat back on Petal's knees holding on to Petal's right hand. Petal was quicker than Flower and pulled hard at the thong. Flower started to get up and Petal used the thong to pull herself out of the mud ripping it off and throwing it to the side of the pool. Flower stood for a moment with her hands covering herself from view, but Petal was intent on mayhem and slid towards her, grasping her round the waist with the intention of taking advantage of Flower's momentary distraction to throw her out of the pool.

Petal had reckoned without Flower having set up the situation and as they met face to face, Flower grasped Petal's thong and tore it until it hung between Petal's legs like a tiny rag. Petal tried to retrieve her situation but Flower slipped behind her and pulled both her arms behind her back. With her free hand she finished the work of destruction which she had started and the audience had the pleasure of seeing two naked, mud-slimed girls before them. The guests had started to take sides, some calling out for Petal and others for

Flower. The action so far had been fast and fierce, but now both girls were completely naked it appeared to be something of a grudge match.

Flower manoeuvred Petal to the ground and trapped her head between her thighs. Petal flailed with her hands catching Flower a blow across the breasts which made the mud fly. Flower edged forward to keep Petal's head between her thighs, but was quite unable to move and made a grab at Petal's right arm. Petal resisted the attempt and replied by opening her mouth and taking Flower's muddy vulva in her mouth. Judging by the scream which Flower produced, Petal had sharp teeth. Flower risked damage by pushing forward so that her bottom covered Petal's face and attempted to quell the flailing arms and now kicking feet. Her position was less effective than she thought and Petal slid out from under her and grasped the kneeling Flower from behind. She carefully inserted a foot between Flower's legs and got her in a head lock. Petal's legs spread apart on the slippery mud and Flower reached back and inserted most of her hand in Petal's vagina. Petal went suddenly quite stiff and stopped moving. Flower leaned back and began to get up, dragging Petal with her. Petal got her legs working as Flower circled her so that they stood face to face with Flower leaning forward so that she could retain her grip within Petal. Petal began to moan and the audience could see, beneath the slick coating of mud, Flower's forearm muscles were working her insides hard. Petal made an attempt to grasp Flower's arm but she was promptly dissuaded by an even more agonising attack on her vagina. Petal stood as if transfixed with her legs apart and her hands behind her head. A hush had descended on the audience.

Flower adjusted her position to ensure a wholly successful grip on Petal, but as she did, Petal immediately penetrated Flower with one hand and drew her close with the other so that she could reach behind Flower and screw her fingers into Flower's rectum. Whatever the agonies that Petal had had to endure these were as nothing compared with what Flower was now going through, and whilst she tried to attack Petal in the same way as she was being penetrated, Petal's reaction was so fierce that she desisted. Slowly Petal drew Flower down into the mud and as she subsided on to her back. Petal removed her hand from Flower's bottom and pressed it against her chest, all the time kneeling between Flower's legs and keeping her hand engaged in Flower's vagina.

Flower appeared to have gone limp, but very shortly it became apparent that Petal's thumb was working on Flower's clitoris and that her fingers had located Flower's G spot. Flower began a slow writhing motion in the mud with her arms thrown back and her chin drawn up so that her neck was strained and she almost looked behind her. Petal was inexorable and pulled at Flower's nipples with her thumb and forefinger as she worked her clitoris. Flower opened her legs wider and moved in the mud. She began to cry out, though whether this was a plea in her native language for Petal to desist, or to keep on, or was just a series of cries of pain and pleasure, it was impossible to say, though the audience soon had a clue as she arched her back and thrust herself against Petal's fearsome little hand. These cries were the mounting chorus of orgasmic pleasure and Petal had no intention of letting her go until she had had more than one orgasm. Eventually Flower screamed out in her second orgasm and her juices mingled with the mud. She lay, supine, her frail chest heaving to take in more breath. Petal turned to the audience and bowed, but she was not quite finished. She knelt in the mud facing the audience and opened her knees. Her left hand reached between her thighs and parted her lips. Her pink and shiny inner lips came out in sharp relief against the dripping mud that covered her. She placed the first two fingers of her right hand against the lips and found her clitoris. Very slowly she began to work her fingers up and down either side of her clitoris as she leaned back thrusting her pelvis out. Flower rose from the mud and stood behind Petal. She placed one hand over Petal's mouth and used her other hand to grasp the delicate button of Petal's nose and prevent her from breathing. Flower began to count as Petal continued with her fingers. At a slowly counted twenty she released her hands for a moment and Petal gasped for breath. At once Flower's hands resumed their stifling of Petal. Flower began to count, slowly again. At twenty five Petal seemed to be in distress, at thirty her fingers increased their speed and at thirty three she appeared to collapse and Flower removed her hands and Petal's heaving chest groped for air and she came with such violence that her juices were forced down her thighs and washed away some of the mud. She knelt with her eyes shut and her unmoving fingers still between her thighs as she slowly keeled over into the mud. Flower bent to hold her neck for a moment and then gently lifted Petal to her feet. The two girls bowed to the audience and received their applause without any sign of pleasure. At the side of the pool, Tania provided Flower with an all enveloping towelling robe which was made like a boiler suit complete with attached feet. Flower went to the shower, dropped the robe beside it and stepped inside, very soon transforming herself into the exquisite creature she had been half an hour before. Petal was recovering at the side of the pool with Tania, whilst Ivan switched on a powerful pump which sucked away almost all of the mud. The audience left their seats and made their way to the bar looking slightly ruffled compared with when they arrived.

Nick and Sarah disappeared into the store room and changed their clothes. Sarah tried pulling the lines of beads over her breasts, but was quite unsuccessful in concealing them. Nick fought against his natural reaction on seeing Sarah partly naked and realised that the leotard that Tania had just given him was of the thinnest material and was very nearly transparent despite its black colour. There was nothing he could do about anything now, but he looked down at himself with some concern.

They peered round the doorway of the store to see that the pool had disappeared and that Petal and Flower were not present. The audience was heavily engaged in consuming powerful drinks as fast as they could manage, and these were already having an effect, judging by the laughter and the people standing very close to each other with hands seeking out things to fondle and the occasional pairs of lips pressed together.

Ivan was calling the audience back to the seats and there seemed no reluctance to be entertained by the second half act. Nick had a momentary flash of panic, but it subsided almost at once.

"Thank you, ladies and gentlemen. I hope you

enjoyed the wrestling and its outcomes. Now I have to introduce you to two newcomers to our salon: Vincent and Sylvie."

There was a ripple of clapping, the house lights dimmed and as they reached the middle of the floor they found themselves illuminated from the sides by a pleasant copper glow. The music started, Sarah stepped away from Nick and raised her arms in a circle above her head. Nick cracked the whip at her feet and she began to dance. The effect was all that she could have wished. The beaded strings swayed and swung with her body, opening across her and revealing her to be naked, but quickly closing again so that there was no chance of a consistent view. The music was slow and languorous and Sarah moved to it with a grace that Nick had not expected. Her early ballet lessons were paying off in quite different circumstances. Sarah swung her hips and the beads moved aside to reveal the full length of her right leg with her breast momentarily fully exposed. As she danced she was goaded on by Nick's cracking whip and she caught a line of beads at each crack of the whip and pulled it into her hand. The music became a little faster in tempo and Sarah started to turn and spin so that the beads flew out from her neck and the audience were treated to an almost full length view of her naked body. Nick continued to crack his whip and Sarah gathered more lines of beads in her hands which she used to emphasise her movements. She could feel herself entering into the spirit of the music and she seemed to float over the floor. There were few of the beads left and she twisted and turned to demonstrate new steps and showed off her nude body to the audience. She turned away from them and pulled off the collar with the remaining beads. She turned towards her viewers when, without warning she seemed to slip and as the music suddenly stopped she fell to one knee and supported herself with both hands on the floor.

Nick uttered an inarticulate cry, but it was clear that he was furious. He cracked the whip close to Sarah who slowly stood up.

Nick shouted at Sarah and she adopted the position with which she had started the dance. Nick wasn't satisfied and flicked her arm with the tip of the whip. Sarah gave a little shake and adjusted her position and began to move across the floor in slow motion. Nick flicked her buttocks and she thrust out her hips provocatively. She did a turn but half way through was checked by the whip against her thigh. She repeated the turn and took three steps towards Nick. He flicked the tip of the whip across her breasts and she uttered a whimper, moving her arms back and raising her breasts in the process.

Sarah danced on at less than half the previous speed and Nick flicked the whip at her and caught her across the back and the belly. She twisted away from the audience and turned her back on them. She bent forward at the hips and Nick cut her across the buttocks where her labia protruded. She at once straightened up and spun slowly away from him, only to receive two cuts to the belly and the back. Nick cracked the whip and Sarah stopped and came towards him. Two metres away and she raised her hands in front of her, as if in supplication. He cracked the whip again and Sarah turned sideways to him folding her hands at the back of her neck. Nick snaked out the whip across the tops of her thighs, and almost without pausing he cut her across the belly and then the navel and next below her breasts and then across her breasts. Sarah uttered a moan of despair and shook her arms making her breasts move rhythmically against one another.

Nick caught her just below the shoulders and then in the middle of her back, round her waist and across her buttocks. Sarah shook and groaned. He cracked the whip again and she turned towards him. Another crack of the whip and Sarah stood on her right foot, lifting her left foot behind her until she caught it in one hand. The other arm stretched out to balance her body as she stood contorted, Nick flicked the whip out and the tip caught Sarah between the thighs, causing her to wobble and cry out. Four more stinging blows were followed by four more cries and the wobble became too much for her to control and she fell to the floor.

Nick cracked the whip again and Sarah arranged herself with her shoulders and head on the floor supported down her body by her arms. She lifted her legs and drew them apart until she was in the position of doing the splits upside down. The audience craned to see her displayed and seemed to be well pleased with what they saw. Nick stood back, and then without warning started to deliver cuts with the whip alternately to each leg starting at Sarah's knees. Sarah raised her legs towards him until her belly was vertically over her face. At each cut of the whip Sarah uttered a cry. Her labia had pulled apart with the effort of her pose and showed her pink inner lips and her clitoris. Nick edged his cuts ever closer to the vulnerable target and Sarah began to shake her legs in agony. At last he struck home against her cunt and Sarah howled and shook and at the third strike juice overflowed from her, ran down her belly and bathed her face. She licked it away from her lips as Nick gave what was to be the last of his cuts which brought her to an as-yet unexperienced agony and a streaming ecstasy. She collapsed to the floor, jerking and writhing, whilst Nick put down the whip and as the audience applauded he bent and picked her up in his arms. Sarah continued to shudder, but began to be quietened by Nick's lips on hers. He put her down gently and stood beside her. As they bowed to the audience he realised that his erection had reached beyond his navel into that part of the leotard which was entirely transparent. He turned away and drew Sarah away with him.

Once they were out of sight, Nick pushed Sarah urgently up against one of the rough walls and fumbled his rampant erection free of his leotard. Sarah was whimpering from combined pain and urgency and she was so wet that he hardly realised he had entered her until he felt her inner muscles clench around him. Then her strong thighs were gripped around him and as he thrust as best he could, she executed a series of controlled rises and falls on the end of his impaling shaft until they both came with shuddering intensity.

*

Afterwards, Nick consoled the still shaking Sarah and soothed her with emollient oils. She began to be easier in herself as he helped her into her clothes and changed into his own. So much had they been involved in their own affairs that they were oblivious to what had been going on in the room behind them. As they emerged they realised that the chairs had gone and with them the audience. Tania and Ivan were sitting on a two seater sofa with Tania half across Ivan's knees. Both of them were looking at Sarah and Nick.

"Come here," Ivan demanded.

"You would like us to provide a critique of your performance?" Tania enquired.

Both Nick and Sarah could think of nothing better than getting a taxi home, engaging in a more gentle massage and falling asleep in their comfortable bed. But this was important and if they were to progress they needed to listen and take notice.

"This was an odd performance," Tania told them. "Sarah started with some titillation in that beaded curtain. At first I didn't think it was a good choice, but the dancing was well done and the view of your body was what they came for. Well, part of what they came for. You were a bit uncomfortable with your pose, Nick. The ladies in the audience were no doubt delighted with the evidence of your fine manhood, but you did nothing with it, and whilst the main interest will always be Sarah, you should be showing off at times to divert interest from her.

"When you got going with the whip you appeared to have only two strokes, a flick which used the tip and a swing which caught Sarah with the last twenty centimetres of the whip. I will teach you much more. I was pleased that you, Sarah, could stand so much pain and that you have no trouble with displaying your body to the audience. However, I think that the whole act needs more drama. For a start, the early music was OK, but you needed something like a beating drum to accompany the whipping. There was something of a lack of ritual about the whole performance, and formalising it makes for a greater impact on the audience. We'll go into that in later lessons."

Ivan added his views. "I'm not so sure about the lifted leg which made you look ungainly. The collapse was all that could follow and was a bit predictable. The inverted splits was interesting, but I don't think it should be the finale. For a start your beautiful body is not as visible to the audience as they would like and it all seemed unlikely that anyone would willingly adopt quite such a contorted position for as long as you did. The orgasm was good, but was not as noticeable as it would have been had you been standing up. Your exit was well managed."

"Oh dear," Nick said, "I'm sorry that you didn't think much of our show,"

"I didn't say that. A beautiful submissive girl and a fine upstanding young man are bound to go down well, and they did. We had a number of very appreciative comments and several people hoped that they would see you again. Our job is to make it better for them, and when that happens it will be better for you."

Tania smiled at them. "You aren't to go away empty handed. The Master hoped that he might see another performance and asked me to give you this."

This was a crisp banker's envelope with a crest at the bottom right hand corner. Nick looked at it with surprise.

"You may open it."

Nick forced his thumb under the flap and looked inside. He took out a slim pack of twenty pound notes.

"Wow, that's nice." He flicked through them. "There are ten." He took the top one off the pile and handed it to Tania. "Ten per cent we agreed, I think."

"Good," said Ivan. "You show an honest and thoughtful spirit. We would have been rather unhappy if you had just taken us for granted, but as it's your first time, and this was intended as a gift rather than payment, you can have your ten percent back."

"That's very kind of you. And of him. How do we say thanks to him?"

"I'm sure there'll be a chance to do that. He's a regular attender here, but next time you will be paid, because you will be worth paying."

"Now you can go home and have a couple of days to recover before we meet again."

"We'll need a taxi."

"No you won't. The Master is very thoughtful and has left you his car and his chauffeur."

*

The journey home was uneventful, but Nick's attempt to discover the identity of their benefactor was swiftly deflected by the chauffeur. Nick told him the number of the house and as they stopped, the chauffeur was immediately out of the car, opened the passenger door and was helping Sarah out. Nick attempted to thank him for his care of them and give him a tip, but the chauffeur refused to accept.

Over the ensuing days Sarah expressed her fears about Ivan, saying that she thought he had no feeling at all for her pain and that had Nick not been always present he might have whipped her until she passed out. Nick disagreed with her and they visited Ivan and Tania and built up their skills and their repertoire. Sarah liked to dance gracefully and seductively and this asset was made much of in their performance. Nick learned to use a number of different whips and practised on models. Tania introduced them to various pieces of stage equipment, all of it designed to show off the victim in the most painful and revealing way. Nick asked if she had ever used some of the equipment and she told him that there was nothing there that hadn't been created just for her, but that not all of it was used at that time and some hadn't been for a long time.

Sarah and Nick continued their existing jobs on the assumption that nothing might come of all their efforts, or that the pay would not be enough to live on. They hadn't an established reputation like Tania and Ivan, nor did they manage other people. However, they were quick learners and enjoyed what they had to take in. Sarah became somewhat frustrated that she wasn't being displayed and punished, but Tania told her that was all to the good because she still wanted what would make her a most desirable attraction and her willingness was an enormous bonus. One evening, whilst Ivan was busy with Nick, Sarah was bursting to ask Tania questions.

"Forgive me asking you, Tania, but are you submissive?"

Tania looked hard at Sarah. "In certain circumstances I will do exactly what I am told and I will not only obey Ivan, I will encourage him to dominate me, and if that means hurting me, that's okay."

"But not all the time?"

"No. That is a pathological state where the submissive needs help."

"I think I might be getting like that."

"Tell me."

"Well, when we've finished work for the day I want Nick to do things to me."

"Oh, I'm just the same. Last night I wanted Ivan to tie my hands together and hook them over the clothes peg on the back of our bedroom door, so that I was completely at his mercy."

Sarah licked her lips, "And what then?"

"Well I must have looked sufficiently attractive for Ivan to follow this up with a good whipping and then..." Tania looked a little dreamy so that Sarah forbore from asking the obvious. "Very shortly we shall have a suggested programme of events for you. They are in the evening or at the weekend so you should be able to fit them in with whatever else you want to do."

Sarah became excited. "Do you think we're ready?"

"Quite ready. You'll find that experience allows you to vary and refine your shows. Your tastes and wishes will change and your shows will change with them. No one can dictate what you should do. Well, no one who is just a paying customer."

"What do you mean?"

"Well, there are opportunities where you can become members of a coterie of like minded people. Many of them are performers. Some will want to have their wishes satisfied, but it has to be with your agreement, though often it is good to try out something impromptu. There can be a lot of satisfaction as well as amusement for everyone, even if it all goes wrong."

"Is this coterie the people we performed for?"

"Some of them."

"Who is the Master?"

"He manages to keep his identity to himself. I often wonder about the hair and the beard. They certainly suit him, but I suspect that they are all part of some elaborate disguise."

"You could trace him from his car registration."

"For a start you'd want to be very intrusive, and his cars are registered in his chauffeurs' names."

"Has he more than one?"

"Indeed so."

"He must be very rich."

"He met us when we were struggling with an act which was little more than an extended strip tease. He suggested changes and we went to his house, or, I should say, one of his houses, and gave a performance for him and a few friends. He was sufficiently pleased to say that we ought to be branching out and perhaps be agents and trainers. This place belonged to him, but he transferred it to us and we have done just what he said ever since. Which is why you are here, and also why he was here at your debut."

"That's why you said we would have a chance to say thank you."

"You will undoubtedly meet again."

The evening progressed. Tania had a word with Ivan who went to the store room and drew out a piece of equipment mounted on a trolley. Sarah, Tania and Nick gathered round it.

"I think that this is one for Sarah." Tania said and smiled at her. "Strip, please, Sarah."

Sarah was filled with anxious anticipation and shed her garments without hesitation.

"This is the sort of thing that you can set up before the performance and push into the arena. The user can be clothed or naked to start off with. Let's see if you fit it, Sarah."

Sarah approached the trolley and Ivan stepped on the wheel brake.

"Turn to face Tania and raise your arms. This is a spreader bar. You can have your arms together or spread out up to at least seventy five degrees. The cuffs slide along the bar and they are secured with a clamp. Let's put your hands through the cuffs. As you can see, Nick, Sarah is standing on the ground. We can now fix her ankles to another bar. Spread your legs a bit, Sarah. Good, that's just how it should be. You'll have noticed, Nick, that the bottom bar is secured to the trolley base whilst the top bar angles in from the vertical pillar. There's plenty of room to walk round her, but both fixings are on revolving joints so that you may move her to face in any direction."

"That's all clever stuff, but Sarah looks a bit slumped to me. Perhaps we should have had a longer pillar. Sarah's taller than Tania and she needs a bit of extra height."

"Let's see what we can do." Ivan pressed his foot on a lever at the side of the trolley and the pillar extended itself by about a centimetre. "That hasn't had much effect. Let's try it again." Ivan pedalled rapidly. The pillar rose and so did the bar to which Sarah was attached. Within a few seconds Sarah was hanging by her arms from the bar, her feet just clear of the trolley. "Does that look better?" Ivan enquired.

"She looks lovely. She always did, but the trips to the gym have toned her beautifully."

"We can improve matters still further. Watch carefully, Nick." Ivan pressed the lever again and the lifting pillar took up the slack in the bottom bar fixing.

"How tall did you say Sarah was, Nick?"

"About 165 centimetres, I think."

"How would you like her to be 167 centimetres?" Without waiting for an answer Ivan pressed down on the pedal and Sarah's arms raised another two centimetres. Her ribs became even more prominent and her body elongated fractionally pulling her bottom in and thrusting her pelvis forward.

Sarah quaked internally, wondering how far Ivan would go with this tearing apart of her vulnerable frame.

"We'll try just a little more."

This time the only place for movement appeared to be in the area of Sarah's belly and crotch. Her pelvis tilted further and she thrust forward her naked vulva with a frightened whimper.

"I'll try you for tension, Sarah," Ivan said and put a hand on each of her hips and pulled and there was virtually no movement.

"That's about as rigid as a human body can stand. This machine is a copy of a traction machine used in Germany during the last war. The action is hydraulic and it is possible to do serious damage with it, which is why I was so careful. We will let Sarah go a little bit so that she can move, within certain bounds." He turned a small wheel on the side of the pillar and the bar began to sink. Quickly he closed the valve. "How much can you move, Sarah?"

Sarah could move her body a little and swing her hips from side to side a few centimetres. Her legs, freed of the ultimate tension, could be moved a little.

"Just a tiny bit more, I think."

Sarah took a deep breath and her ribs showed white beneath her skin and the arch of her ribs at the bottom of the rib cage became even more prominent.

"That's beautiful," said Tania, "you are just about perfect to be a victim. Can you stand it?"

"Of course," she replied, wondering what was to follow.

"Now, Nick, turn her round."

The effect was as beautiful as the front view, with Sarah's back presented to them and the tight, high globes of her buttocks completing the slender length of her back.

"Here we go, then," said Ivan as he handed Nick a short wooden handle to which had been attached a dozen or so slender strands of leather about fifty centimetres long, the dreaded 'cat', but without knots or barbs. Tania sat over to the right of Nick and to his front so that he could see her with a drumstick in her hand and a drum in front of her. She raised the stick and Nick managed almost perfect timing with the cat descending across Sarah's shoulders as the sound issued from the drum. Sarah shook a little in her cuffs and Nick realised why Ivan had made it possible for her to show a reaction by movement. The next strike was a little lower on her back and Nick could see Tania counting to herself between each beat of the drum. He followed suit and made it a count of five. From then on it was easy to keep the beating of the drum and Sarah in perfect harmony.

Nick striped Sarah's bottom with a criss-cross of weals, though so far he had used no more than the warming up strength. He caught Sarah at the top of her thighs, but though she swung a little there was no sign that he was hurting her unbearably. After another three blows, Sarah managed to turn herself in the machine and faced Nick and Ivan. It was the signal for a rather more brutal attack. The first blow spread out across her belly as did the second. This time Sarah threw back her head and cried out, audible even above the sound of the drum. Nick struck again, at first just below her breasts and then across them. Sarah shrieked and he repeated his attention to the same target. Sarah twisted and tried to turn, jiggling her tortured breasts against each other and moving her pelvis backwards and forwards. Out of the corner of his eye he saw Ivan pointing, and following the direction of his gesture saw that he was drawing attention to a slight, slick, shine on Sarah's thighs. He struck her across the top of the thighs, on the belly and again across her breasts. Sarah's movements were more pronounced and she drew back her pelvis as far as it could go and then thrust it forward with her breasts moving in unison. Sarah was again entering into the spirit of the adventure, deep within her there was an insistent voice telling her to avoid the display of her nakedness and to stop being a tortured victim. She silenced the voice by looking down at her naked breasts and watching the cat spread over them.

At the next beat of the drum Nick swept the cat up between Sarah's legs and caught her across the vulva. Sarah howled like a wounded dog, but Nick followed up the attack and watched the muscles on Sarah's belly ripple, her mouth open and then the inevitable gush of juices which signalled the fulfilment of her orgasm. She shook and cried out at the same time as Nick undid the valve on the column and the bar descended so that her feet touched the ground.

Nick tore at the Velcro fastenings and caught Sarah as she was about to crumple to the floor. He carried her to the sofa, laying her on it and covering her with a soft blanket. She caught his hand, kissed it and whispered "Thank you."

Sarah seemed to drift off into a slightly uneasy sleep. Nick listened to what Tania and Ivan had to say and had the wit to take notes. Sarah began to stir. Nick went over to her with a bottle of Tania's favourite salve and started to apply it, massaging Sarah in a quiet, gentle and apparently seductive way. She had been lying on her front and she turned towards him and reached up her arms. Ivan and Tania were nowhere to be seen. Nick reached down and cradled the softness of a breast, squeezing the nipple between his fingers. Sarah pulled his face down to hers and groaned her pleasure into his ear. She turned herself over and parted her legs enough to allow Nick's hand to slip down her stomach and bury itself in the warmth and moisture between her thighs. His fingers slipped easily inside her as her fingers began to fumble urgently with his trousers.

*

Several days passed before Nick received a phone call from Ivan and that evening he and Sarah presented themselves to their managers.

"We hope you haven't a lot of other engagements because we think that the time has come for you to start earning and for us to benefit from your income. You will always be paid in cash, but in future we will accompany you to the venues and the cash will be paid to us. We will deduct our ten per cent and give you the rest. On most of these occasions we, too, will be performing, so that we will need to ensure we don't do anything like the same thing. Then there's six weeks tomorrow when we have a meeting of the little club we mentioned. What you will have to do there will be requested by the membership. However, there is a proviso that whoever gets to tell you what to do has to pay you and, in case you're wondering, the choosers are required to bid what they are prepared to pay for what they want you to do and the highest bid wins. They can sometimes be quite generous and you get to keep it all. You may get an invitation to join the club, and if you do it's well worth joining. The Master is the chairman and he arranges the venues."

Tania produced two pages of A4 paper. She gave one to Nick and Sarah and shared hers with Ivan.

There appeared to be two venues each week on Wednesday and Saturday nights. A thought crossed Sarah's mind.

"Tania, what if I'm.."

"Menstruating? No problem, we have a gimmick that allows you to bleed as part of the performance."

"Aren't people put off by that?"

"Not the way we do it. You'll find it a positive advantage to give your Tampax a rest. Besides we find that the stimulus of a good whipping ensures that things speed up and more happens in an evening than usually does in two or three days. Then it's all over."

They arranged when and where to meet and planned out the specific shows for the first fortnight.

"You won't have any bother with nerves because you've already performed in front of an audience, and a much more difficult one than these will be. People are quite easily pleased provided they see plenty of naked bodies and evidence that the pain is real."

"I always want to be made love to at the end of a whipping," Sarah confessed.

"Oh, good. We'll have a plant in the audience who tells Nick to do just that, and you should do it, like the display and the whipping, entirely for your own pleasure. If you are enjoying it, so will the audience."

"So anything goes?"

"Pretty much. We meet here on Saturday at 4 p.m."

*

Saturday morning dawned dull and wet. Nick rolled over in bed and drew Sarah towards him.

"I'd like a fuck," she said, "but remember the plant in the audience. You wouldn't want to let them down."

"No chance of that."

"Even so, I'd like you to be rampant and ravishing rather than quiet and working on it. Mind you that is a hard-on to remember. But waiting a bit will do you the world of good."

The day passed relatively slowly as they waited for their first public show. They checked the contents of their props bags several times and then it was time to be off to Ivan and Tania's.

They all got into the Range Rover and crammed into as little space as they could manage in order to make room for the equipment which Ivan had stowed in the car earlier. The journey out of London was relatively easy and by five o'clock they had arrived at the gates of an isolated country house. The gatekeeper checked their identity and opened the electric gates with his remote control. They parked close to the front of the house and three men dressed in dark suits appeared.

"Is it all this in the back?" one of them enquired and

in a twinkling the back of the car was empty and they walked to the front steps with their bags. They were admitted at once and Tania handed over the keys to the car. A man in his mid-thirties approached them.

"Before I take you to your rooms, I'll show you the theatre."

Though this was a private house it contained a small theatre with raked seats and a couple of boxes, unusually sited so that the occupants had an excellent view of the stage,

The stage itself was almost as big as the auditorium and was quite low in relation to the audience, none of whom, even in the front rows, would have had to crane their necks to see everything which transpired. There was a sophisticated lighting set and the exit and entry points were well disguised by draperies. They mounted the stage and went to the back where there was a corridor with dressing room doors off it. The second one was for Sarah and Nick, the third for Ivan and Tania.

Sarah and Nick went into theirs and were pleased to find a sizeable room with a bathroom at the end. The make up desk was very well lit and had a wide selection of paints and creams on it, together with a lobster salad, coffee in a big vacuum dispenser and an array of alcoholic and soft drinks. It was evident that performers were to be separated from audience, but were to be treated well. Sarah went next door to consult Tania.

"It'll start dead on seven. There'll be a warm-up act and then you will be called. You'll find the stage has been prepared for you. I sent details of exactly what we wanted a week ago and it will all be just as we asked. You should take about half an hour, a bit longer if our plant shouts loudly," Tania laughed. "There'll be lots of drink flowing and then it's our turn. We should be over by eight thirty and they'll be very pleased to see us go while they all get on with their business."

"What business is that?"

"Drinking, and what passes for love making among the wealthy classes."

"Do we know who the warm up act is?"

"No, but never mind, we'll be able to watch from the wings if we want to."

Sarah decided she would very much like to watch and told Nick. At a little after six they changed into their costumes. Nick's was simple: a thong too small to cover his erection if he had one, and a patterned Karate Gi. Sarah's costume was similarly simple. She put on a black G string followed by what looked like a Gi but in some shimmering, virtually transparent material, but not likely to be quite transparent enough to satisfy the audience.

Nick kept glancing nervously at the clock and at 7 p.m. there was a knock at their door and Tania, dressed in an all concealing dressing gown, beckoned them to the wings of the stage. They looked out at the audience, most of whom were quite informally dressed, and who appeared to be doing their best to drink themselves into a state where their inhibitions were totally dulled. As they watched the house lights were dimmed and extinguished and an amplified voice bid them welcome Peter and Jane. Two bodies pressed past the watchers and ran on to the stage. They were dressed in leather harnesses and carried whips. Jane turned on Peter as he came towards her and started to flail at him with her whip, in exchange Peter leaped back out of her immediate range and returned the compliment. They started to trade blow for blow, attempting to strike home at delicate parts of each other's bodies, but parried by the other's whip. Sarah realised that she was watching a whip fight, something she had never even thought of before. Every so often a heavy blow landed on an opponent and there was a cry of pain. The action was fast and furious and without let up. Slashing whips seemed to be everywhere, but Sarah noticed that neither of them managed to get in blows which would bring an advantage which could be followed up. She decided that it was all rather cleverly done and wondered at the speed at which they moved and the number of blows that they aimed. Someone in the audience called out for Jane 'to give it to him' and someone else shouted in support of Peter.

The whips tangled and Peter had his pulled out of his hand and dropped on the floor. As he bent to retrieve it Jane slashed repeatedly at his back and his buttocks and Peter scrambled away quickly, unexpectedly cracking the whip against Jane's belly as he did so. Jane let out a cry and came back into the fight with redoubled violence. The couple were using every bit of the quite large stage and their act was a testimony to their fitness as well as their ability to wield the whips and their strength in recovering from the occasions when a hit was landed. Sweat was running down their faces and over their bodies and Peter had a very obvious erection. Jane shortened her grip on her whip and came in slashing at Peter who parried her blows with his whip, as they broke away from one another Peter caught her a momentarily paralysing blow to the cunt and Jane stopped in her tracks and as she crumpled to her knees with her hands between her legs. Peter slashed at her mercilessly. Standing astride her and cutting at her with his whip, covering her upper body with weals. Jane rolled on to her back to protect herself and he repeated the pattern of attack. She raised her arms to protect herself but as she did so Peter slashed repeatedly at the thin leather cover of her crotch and she turned over again on to her hands and knees with her head down. Peter pulled her up by her hair and gave her half a dozen vicious cuts to her crotch and breasts.

The fight was at an end and as Jane slowly struggled to her feet, Peter raised his whip in a gesture of triumph. They bowed to the audience whose applause was enthusiastic. They turned and walked off the stage hand in hand, not speaking to Tania or Sarah who both complimented them on their act.

"That was something else," said Sarah.

"Oh yes, indeed. But you'll notice that the fetish harness broke up the blows a bit. Peter certainly had an erection, but neither of them showed the audience a great deal. That bra may have exposed her nipples, but you saw precious little of her breasts. Still, it's basically a good idea and we might try it for real," Ivan told her.

Sarah shivered at the idea.

The audience had returned to its affairs and Sarah and Nick watched as the stage was prepared for them. What had seemed a brief period of activity by Jane and Peter had been the better part of twenty minutes. The lights dimmed again and then went out and the disembodied voice announced Vincent and Sylvie.

They went hand in hand onto the stage and bowed to the audience. They turned to each other and bowed. Their first movements were bending and stretching and then stepping from one foot to the other. They raised their arms above their heads and made them into windmills. They stepped back from each other, sideways on to the audience and bowed again. Sarah adopted the fighter's classic defence position and Nick sought to penetrate her defences with a series of moves, but Sarah was always too fast for him. She successfully landed a passing kick halfway up his thigh and then slipped behind him and tried to disable him from the rear. Nick was wise to this manoeuvre and slipped away from her. The fight progressed for several minutes until they came to grappling. They started with their fingers intertwined and at once Nick made use of his superior strength and forced Sarah to her knees. With a swift movement Sarah disengaged herself from Nick's grasp and moved away from him. Nick reached out to her as she turned but only managed to grasp the neck of her Gi. Sarah started to turn but Nick hung on and the Gi opened at the front and was pulled off Sarah's shoulders, leaving her naked to the waist. There was a small ripple of applause, though this seemed tame stuff after all the action with the whips. Sarah flung herself at Nick who found himself with his Gi trousers at knee level and a fighting Sarah seizing his wrist and bending it back behind him. Trapped by his ankles Nick kicked off the trousers whilst trying to disentangle himself from Sarah. He fell heavily on his back and Sarah at once straddled him as he lay, face up and breathing heavily. She had caught his right arm under her left knee and was twisting his left arm with both of hers.

Nick arched his back but Sarah hung on. Nick tried to bring his arm close to his chest, but Sarah was having none of it and continued to try to twist his arm into a surrender. Nick, in one flowing movement, brought up his knees to Sarah's back and then drove them down again pulling up his body by the counterweight and toppled Sarah off his chest. He sprang to his feet, but she was there before him and had got behind him and was attempting a headlock.

Nick reached round behind him and attempted a crushing move with both arms round Sarah's waist and his wrists grasped in his hands. Before he had a chance to complete the move Sarah had danced away from him giving him a neat kick on the side of his chest and leaving him with her trousers, torn from waist to hems in his hand. Sarah looked magnificent. Her beautiful figure was enhanced by the splendid muscles she had acquired over many weeks in the gym. She was lithe and fast and knew the moves. Her tiny black G string seemed to accentuate rather than cover her nakedness. Nick rushed at her, the jacket of his Gi flapping. He tried a grasping move to enfold her in his arms, but Sarah was too quick for him, gave him a powerful kick in passing and twisted him round with his own jacket and pulled it off one shoulder.

Nick tried to shrug the jacket back on but the diversion of his attention led Sarah to move behind him and pull him off balance. Nick took two paces to try to regain his balance, but Sarah grasped his jacket and pulled it down to his waist whilst kicking him behind the right knee. As he went down, Sarah pulled the Gi off his back and gave him a two footed kick which threw him on his side. She at once straddled him again, but this time Nick's arm wasn't trapped and he was able to seize both her arms in his hands and lever her off him. Sarah sprawled on the padded floor and at once Nick was on his feet. The close proximity of Sarah and his unstoppable desire for her manifested itself in half his rigid penis showing above his thong. He turned to her and she was just an iota too late to avoid his grasp. He caught her arms in his hands and twisted them behind her back, holding her so that she faced the audience with her whole body drawn into tension. He dropped to one knee and pulled her over his thigh so that her legs were on one side and her body lay arched backwards. Sarah groaned.

Nick had become slightly careless, thinking he had a submission, and seemed absolutely unprepared for Sarah's fingers groping at his thong and grasping a testicle. She squeezed and Nick howled, dropping his grip on her and rolling her off his thigh. Sarah performed a very neat sideways roll and ended up on her feet. Before he could recover, Sarah had kicked him expertly in the crotch. Perhaps the pain was so awful this time that Nick had to do something about it. Sarah had begun to turn away in triumph when she felt Nick's arm round her throat. She reached back, but Nick pressed himself against her and she did no more than catch the strap of his thong in her fingers. In desperation she tore at this whilst Nick pressed his free hand down her belly and engaged her G string. Their timing was perfect bringing them both to nudity at the same moment. Nick twisted Sarah round until she was facing him and enveloped her in a bear hug. Sarah's lungs began to protest and she drew a rasping gulp of breath. Nick put a forearm under her buttocks and lifted her from the floor. Half way through the manoeuvre, Sarah twisted in his clutches and ended up facing the audience so that they got their first unimpeded view of her naked body. Nick placed a large hand over her crotch and she opened her legs so that his practised fingers sank into her. The audience gave an approving cheer and Sarah leaned back against Nick with one arm across his shoulder.

The signal that they awaited came from the audience: 'Fuck her!' followed by several others which encouraged Nick to give her a good whipping and fuck her. He carried Sarah to a pair of cuffs which hung at the end of a rope clipping each wrist into a cuff and securing the Velcro. As he did so the rope came under tension and Sarah was left with just her toes on the ground.

The shouts from the audience became insistent: 'Whip her, whip her, whip her!' Nick selected an eight foot whip from a rack and cracked it at the audience which fell silent in anticipation. Sarah looked wonderful with her body stretched out and her breasts rolling together, her narrow waist and the flaring hips with slender legs which seemed impossibly long. She felt the first cut across her belly, followed up by another just below the ribs and another across her buttocks as Nick moved to her side. She cried out at each cut and as they proceeded she started to dance in her agony and Nick flicked the tip of the whip first at one nipple and then at the other and then at her crotch. She opened her legs to feel the bite of the whip and Nick didn't disappoint her. The audience roared their delight and Nick plied the whip willingly all over Sarah's body and occasionally between her legs. Sarah was beginning to leak juice, her head was back and her mouth open, her neck straining to take in the breath which was expelled from her as the cuts took their toll of her resistance.

"Fuck her, fuck her, fuck her!" the audience shouted. Nick tore open the Velcro and Sarah started to slip, but steadied herself with her arms round his neck. Nick showed her off to the audience and turned her round. Her body began to fold and her buttocks pressed against his rampant cock. Nick drew back enough to show the audience his erection and then guided it into her dripping vagina. Sarah moaned, the audience cheered. Nick held on to Sarah's hips plunging deeper and deeper into her. Slowly Sarah moved her body up and rested her weight using her hands on her knees. Nick moved her round so that the audience could see her face and her superb breasts rolling and swinging as he slammed into her. Suddenly, she stood upright and howled a great orgasmic cry. Nick thrust himself deep into her and then withdrew with a fountain of jism spurting from his cock. The audience went wild.

Sarah and Nick made it back to their dressing room with the applause ringing in their ears. Tania was already there pouring champagne and preparing the salad. Ivan was smiling a broad and approving smile.

"Brilliant!" said Tania, "as good a debut as anyone has seen and more than that lot deserved. Mind you, following that isn't going to be easy."

Tania kissed and hugged Sarah and hugged Nick and left them. It was wind down time. A quick shower, a liberal application of the soothing oils and they both began to feel a return to that boring state of normal. They put on their street clothes and heard Ivan and Tania being called.

"We ought to watch," Nick told Sarah.

"I don't think so. After all, we know how good they are and I need a rest."

Nick was happy to go along with her wishes. He kissed Sarah delicately on the lips. After a while she seemed to doze off, but then suddenly awoke.

"I'm hungry."

After they had eaten they crept into the wings to see Tania and Ivan receiving the audience's applause. As they left the stage Tania told Sarah that they would be ready to go in a quarter of an hour.

Sarah wondered if there was a way out other than through the audience. Her question was answered by the sight of a figure walking up the dressing room corridor from the opposite direction to the stage. He knocked at the third dressing room door and Ivan opened it. Something was passed between the two of them and the figure retreated as quietly and unobtrusively as it had come.

Only a few minutes later they were soon travelling south at a much greater speed than on the outward journey. Tania seemed a bit distant, which Nick and Sarah put down to her needing a lot of contact with Ivan, which had not been possible owing to the overriding desire to be back home. The car stopped outside their house and Nick and Sarah were about to alight and collect their bags when Ivan twisted in his seat.

"Not so fast, you two. This was a business arrangement and you haven't been paid yet." He fetched an envelope from his inside pocket. Nick read 'Vincent and Sylvie' in beautiful script on the front. Ivan tore open the envelope with his thumb nail, reached inside and drew out three twenty pound notes. He handed the envelope to Sarah. "The rest is yours and the first of many more. Tonight's was not a very generous venue, but there will be worse and a good many that are better."

Thanks and good nights were exchanged and a time fixed for them to be picked up for the next gig.

Once in their lounge, Nick slid the rest of the notes out of the envelope. There was over five hundred pounds and even though Sarah was yawning they stayed up long enough to plan a strategy for investing their future earnings

*

Weeks passed and one show followed another. In one week they did three shows, having taken over from Ivan and Tania when Tania had an awful cold and couldn't stop coughing. The money rolled in and was put away in safe places. Ivan reminded them of the meeting with the club which was less than a week away.

"I've got the winning bid here, and you'll be very pleased with it when you get the envelope. It's time for you to be buying gold and salting it away in some bank vault. A safety deposit box is a very useful place to put some bullion."

Nick was delighted with the idea and asked Ivan where gold could be bought. Ivan let him into a number of interesting secrets which would secure their financial future. Nick kept quiet about his present arrangements. He was aware that from nothing they were now building capital and had enjoyed themselves a great deal.

Ivan turned the conversation back to the club venue. "These are quite different people from those you've dealt with up to now. These people know what they want and are determined to get it so you will become their agents and do your absolute best for them, no holds barred."

Given their track record up to that point, both Nick and Sarah wondered what no holds barred inferred.

"The winning bid was for Thanatos."

Both Sarah and Nick looked quizzically at Ivan. Tania looked from one to the other.

"Well, that certainly gives them an opportunity for a wonderful exhibition."

"We don't know what it is," Sarah admitted.

"Then I'll tell you. But I will also warn you that no rehearsal is to take place. This must be as fresh and original as possible."

"But we'll have to choose costumes," Nick pointed out.

"Not even that. Everything you need will be provided on the night and you will have separate dressing rooms so that the first time you see each other will be on the stage. You will receive instructions on exactly what to do in your dressing rooms. I think you will be amazing."

"I hope so," Sarah said, rather doubtfully.

Another two shows were followed by a three day lay off and then Ivan and Tania appeared at their door ready to take them to the venue. A curious quiet pervaded the journey time and Nick and Sarah held hands rather apprehensively.

At the door they were separated from one another and led to dressing rooms. "We shall call for you at five minutes to eight," each of them was told, and with that they were left alone to spend an hour and a half reading the instructions and preparing themselves for the forthcoming event. Sarah examined her costume and tried it on. It was an almost backless evening dress in delicate chiffon, cut low at the front to reveal most of her breasts and almost down to her navel and secured by what looked like a single thread of silk which blended into her skin tone and went round the back of her neck. The skirt was of the same diaphanous material and appeared to have been little more than tacked to the top half of the dress. It had a number of slits in it which went from hem to what would have been the waist band and as she walked about in it revealed her long legs perfectly. There was a pair of high-heeled, lightweight court shoes which matched the dress and threw her pelvis forward as she moved in them. She read the instructions several times and picked up the whip which had been provided. This was a hefty weapon of plaited hide with a fine cord at the tip with a small ball of what looked like silver in a cobweb of strands dangling from it. Sarah had had little practice with a whip and decided to try out her skills which rapidly improved after a disastrous start.

Meanwhile Nick was examining his costume which was created from very fine black cotton straps leading down between his legs where a pouch was supposed to hide his sex. He thought of Sarah and at once proved how inadequate the item was. The straps, one of which encircled his waist, were connected to each other by what looked like a single stitch. He handled the ensemble with care. He looked at the whip that he had been given and found a beautifully balanced, lightweight, flexible leather strip with a divided tip. He swished it about him to get the feel of the implement and thought that he would have to put a good deal of effort into ensuring that Sarah felt an adequate amount of pain. He sat on a chair in front of the make up mirror and read the instructions. He was sure there was nothing there he couldn't cope with and wondered what all the fuss was about. A simple bit of posing and each of them alternately having a go at the other didn't seem very exciting. Were these people really connoisseurs? If so they should have attended some of their recent shows which seemed to him to be far more adventurous than this appeared to be.

Promptly at seven fifty five there was a knock on the door and the smart man who had shown him to his dressing room beckoned to Nick.

They came to the wings of the stage and the man whispered, "Wait for the introduction and then walk on to the stage. You know what to do."

Nick couldn't make Sarah out on the opposite side of the stage and wondered what she was wearing. The announcement came: "Ladies and gentlemen, Sylvie and Vincent will perform Thanatos."

Nick walked forward to see Sarah emerge from the opposite drapes. She looked like an under dressed celebrity out of the weekly glossies. The audience was silent. Sarah suspended her whip on a hanger at her waist and faced Nick, putting her hands behind her head. Here was a target which he would have no problem dealing with. He lashed out a single blow which caught Sarah about the level of her waist. She showed no sign of being put out and Nick determined to use more strength next time.

It was Sarah's turn and she caught Nick, who had echoed her pose, across the top of his right thigh with her first lash and then under his left arm with her second. This was a serious weapon, however inexpertly handled and Nick felt the contact instantly.

He waited for Sarah to pose and lashed at her three times with his strap. Her clothing billowed as he struck her and the increased power made her wince, but she remained silent.

Sarah looked at Nick in his ineffectual straps and insufficient cache sexe and walked round him before lashing him. According to the rules they had both read in their rooms, she had four lashes at her disposal and caught him four cuts across the back and buttocks. Nick drew in his breath and Sarah noticed that his erection had wilted.

Nick felt a tiny edge of resentment and caught Sarah across the back with his first blow followed by another at about waist level and a third in which the divided tip of his whip became entangled in the material and as he drew back for the fourth blow the whip tore the material. The fifth caught her across the belly and did more damage to her skirt.

Sarah remembered the instructions: 'Any sign of less than full strength in each blow will result in an exchange of whips and fifty cuts from the opponent." There was a lot more which indicated that the whole thing was a test of their readiness to join the club. She caught Nick across the belly with her first blow and the silver ball twisted in a strap and separated it from the others. The second and third were delivered in quick order and fell across Nick's chest and were followed by three not very successful attempts to catch his groin. Nonetheless the pain was evident, despite Nick's desire to conceal it.

Nick had seven strikes in hand and was determined to make them count. His first blow caught Sarah just below her breasts and did further damage to her dress. The second was aimed at the same target but missed it and pulled a strip of material from what little there was of the side of the dress. The third struck Sarah's navel and pulled some of the skirt out of its tacking. His fourth and fifth strikes were almost vertical and were aimed at ripping the skirt. In this Nick was quite successful, but little more of Sarah was revealed than had been apparent before. The last two in the series were across Sarah's back, but she was inured to such pains and ignored them. Nick started to fear Sarah's next attack, but almost before he made himself ready, a cutting blow fell across his chest. The tip of the whip tangled with his straps and she tore several away as she prepared for the next blow which was to Nick's belly. He emitted a quiet groan and felt more of his costume destroyed by Sarah's whip. Another blow caught his buttocks and he had to remember that whilst he was the victim he had to stand perfectly still, whatever the pain and his inclination. Sarah lashed him across the back and promptly followed it up with a cut across the shoulders. Before he could recover she slashed him twice near the top of his thighs and then, either accidentally or luckily a blow fell on Nick's crotch and ripped his thong away from its supporting straps. He had lost his erection and someone in the audience jeered.

Nick's resentment that he was being cut about with such vigour and with so much pain was substantially increased by the jeering at the miserable winkle between his legs. He knew that this was a turning point in the bout. He shrugged off the remaining straps and stood naked on the stage. He measured Sarah and brought the whip down across her front and buried the tip in the folds of her dress. He pulled as hard as he could at the material and had the satisfaction of seeing the skirt come away from its flimsy tacking and slide to Sarah's feet. The top of the dress continued to cover Sarah down to just below her crotch but he was determined to rip the garment from Sarah's body so that he could expose her to the audience and then whip her into the submission that would end the act.

It took Nick's entire share of blows to achieve his aim and he knew that the now naked Sarah would hurt him. Nothing he couldn't handle, he thought, but he realised that he disliked the pain intensely and resented being beaten by Sarah. She caught him twice across the buttocks which made him push his crotch out, and twice across the shoulders. Her next cuts were to his chest and then, to his dismay, to his crotch. Fortunately for him Sarah misjudged the distance and the thicker part of the whip fell across his penis. Nonetheless, the last cuts evoked a groan from Nick and he bent slightly at the waist as if to alleviate his agony.

Then it was his turn again and he struck Sarah hard across the buttocks, causing her to quiver, another hard blow in the same place produced a small explosive outrush of breath, but Nick slashed her across the belly and then the breasts several times, setting them rolling together. He tried an upward slash to her crotch, but Sarah's knees were pressed together and she missed the pain that this would have inflicted. Filled now with fury and frustration Nick slashed at Sarah indiscriminately until a voice commanded him to stop. He stood still and suddenly Sarah had her shoes removed and a blindfold was placed over her eyes. At the same time Nick was also blindfolded.

Two words were addressed to them: "Now fight."

In the claustrophobic darkness, Nick swung his whip at where he thought Sarah was but the lash whistled harmlessly through thin air. At the same time he felt the wind of Sarah's lash just missing him. He drew his whip back just as her second shot in the dark caught him a blow on the hip. He replied with a flurry of blows some of which, much to his satisfaction, connected with Sarah, he felt the flashy impact of the lashes and hoped he was hurting her. In his mind's eye he saw her delicious breasts wobble and roll as they were whipped. Sarah got lucky with a slash that caught Nick across his belly. The action became much faster, if less accurate and effective. Nick thought that Sarah had stepped back on the stage and having some idea from her blows where she was, moved towards her. He had not taken into account that she had shortened her grip on her whip and he collided with her. Suddenly the touch of her naked body and particularly her breasts brought back Nick's erection and the audience applauded.

Nick, now rampant and no longer insecure, flailed the air until he managed to achieve a strike whilst Sarah caught him across the waist and he jumped in the air and redoubled his efforts to quell her. By chance he swung his arm round and instead of the whip connecting with Sarah's body, his forearm caught her across the side of the head and she fell, senseless, at his feet. He stumbled over her body and at once snatched off his blindfold and cradled her in his arms. A neatly dressed silver haired woman appeared at his side.

"I'm a doctor, I don't think there's much harm done, but it's as well to check."

Sarah began to come round and they removed her blindfold and carried her to a large, comfortable sofa and covered her with a merino rug of comforting warmth and lightness.

"Nothing to worry about, there," he was told. "You better go back on stage."

Reluctantly, Nick left Sarah and returned to the stage. The master of ceremonies was about to present him with a fine silver plate in honour of his victory, when there was a shout from the audience.

"Not so fast! Thanatos is to be decided by whips, not by a clumsy blow from an arm. I demand the right to match my skill against Vincent and we shall then see who wins."

There was a general sound of approval for this suggestion, though Nick felt apprehensive, both at having to face another opponent and also at the possibility of losing. A cheer greeted the speaker and the master of ceremonies introduced Nick to Heidi. He was amazed that his opponent was another woman and wondered what the procedure was going to be.

"Cumulative rounds alternately," was the order. Nick felt foolish and embarrassed at being naked in front of this striking brunette. Heidi looked him up and down.

"None of this messing about with ripping clothes off," she said to him and to suit action to words pulled off her outer garments and kicked off her shoes until she was naked except for a flesh coloured thong. Involuntarily Nick produced evidence of his appreciation of her splendid curves, much to the amusement of the audience.

"Start with a kiss!" Was shouted from the audience and there was much stamping of feet in support. Heidi approached him, reached an arm round his neck, pressed her amazing body against him from the knees to the shoulders and stuck her tongue into his mouth. Nick hesitated for only a moment, feeling his cock twitching against her belly and her breasts against his chest, and mixed his tongue with hers. For a moment the audience was silent and then began to cheer. Nick was appalled at how much he was enjoying the sensation. As they broke Heidi whispered, "No holds barred and the winner gets the girl. For a while." Nick had no idea what this meant, or even if he had heard what she was saying aright.

As he stepped back Heidi ripped at him across the thighs with her whip and he uttered a yelp of pain and surprise. In the moment of his recovery Heidi had moved away and was standing with her hands behind her head and balanced on her toes in the classic receiving position. The pose lifted her splendid breasts with their dark areola and prominent nipples and stretched her body taut, highlighting her muscles all the way to her calves. Whatever it took, Nick was going to subdue this woman. He cut at her across the belly and then the breasts. She produced the tiniest of shivers, noticeable only because her breasts moved.

It was Nick's turn and the first two cuts fell across his chest and then his belly and the third caught his rigid penis and the tip of the whip did two thirds of a circle round it. Nick snorted, but realised that he was beginning to be inured to the pain. In any event there was none of the emotional involvement with this woman and resentment was banished in favour of a determination to win.

Nick found that Heidi was ready for his attentions and he used his ration of blows on her back and buttocks. Heidi had slight difficulty keeping her balance, but showed no other signs of being upset by his attack. Her barrage was swift and accurate and left him gulping for breath. Her last cut caught him across the scrotum and a fearful feeling of nausea and pain spread up his belly. He realised that he would have to do something to reach a turning point in this contest; he feared what might have happened if the last cut had come earlier and been followed by another.

He saw that Heidi had planted her feet a bit apart so as to get a better balance. His first blow was across her waist, the next ones cut at her breasts making her jerk backwards slightly. As she did so he brought the whip up between her thighs and caught her stingingly across her vulva. He still had a blow in hand and repeated the cut. Heidi drew in her belly and gasped out an explosion of air. Nick thought he was certainly doing the right thing. Then he noticed that her left breast was oozing something slightly sticky from the nipple and that her thighs were becoming slick with juice issuing on to them. One way or another, he thought, he would finish it at the next round.

Nick drew himself up to receive Heidi's flurry of blows, but there was a pause before a single cut struck his still erect penis. Nick gasped, expecting an immediate tattoo, but Heidi was measuring him again and then suddenly she was at him and a whistling slash caught his scrotum followed by another and then another. The pain was insupportable. Nick began to buckle at the knees and another two cuts completed the work. As he went down on his knees Heidi utilised her victor's privilege of lashing at Nick's body time and time again. Nick fell forward and then rolled on to his back. Heidi mercilessly cut into his belly and his balls until all that Nick could see or sense was a red fire enveloping him.

In the midst of his agony Heidi stood across him and as if in slow motion Nick felt a warm splash on his chest and then another and looked up to see Heidi's saturated thong dripping on him. This was a woman who got her kicks from domination rather than submission.

The audience had been clapping and cheering for several minutes. An almost incomprehensible shout came over the noise, followed by another and then the audience began to shout "Screw him, screw him, screw him." Heidi reached down and seized Nick by the balls and cock. He was recovering from the torture inflicted on him so recently and managed little more than an unenthusiastic groan. Heidi pulled off her thong and sat on Nick's chest, facing the audience. She shifted her grasp and started to rub his cock up and down until it became rigid. She edged forward and sat on the erection and began moving up and down, gripping Nick's cock with her pelvic floor muscles. Nick realised that this was being done purely for the enjoyment of the audience, but he struggled to move so that his hands and arms were free and he grasped a breast in each hand, realising how big and solid they were. He managed to tweak Heidi's nipples as she sank her fingers into her vulva and exercised her clitoris. Nick found that his fingers were becoming sticky with the issue from her nipples and he could feel the dripping from her vagina. He quickly altered his position so that he was kneeling behind Heidi who was on all fours. He brought his hand down across her buttocks with a loud slap and shoved his cock into her dripping cunt, Heidi struggled at this unexpected change of events, but was constrained by the depth of Nick's penetration and the presence of his large hands griping her breasts. Nick felt the customary twinge of his prostate which presaged his orgasm and realised that Heidi was shaking and bouncing against him whilst mouthing the most remarkable obscenities. She came before he did and he was able to jerk that last three or four times which made him spurt into her. Within a few seconds Heidi had rolled away from Nick with juice and jism streaming down her legs and had bowed to the appreciative audience. She collected her clothes and made her way out to the back of the stage. Nick followed her and made his way to his dressing room. He pushed open the door but found that he was not alone.

Ivan was standing to one side of the make up mirror whilst the Master was sitting in front of it. More than anything else Nick wanted a shower, to put on his clothes and then to fetch Sarah, to whom he thought he might have to do some serious explaining. Instead he stood there, naked and well thrashed, sticky from Heidi and himself, and felt awkward about what to do with his hands.

"You put on a good show tonight," the Master told

him, "but you lost in the battle of the whips, despite your noble reversal of what Heidi intended for you at the end. It's always good to see a triumphant woman howling on the end of a man's cock. There is a forfeit for losing at whips."

Nick remained silent, his current position was sufficiently humiliating without further unpleasantness.

"You must understand that what I am about to tell you is subject to your earnest wish to become a member of our club," the Master said. "The club is not without its resources and tonight's little episode will make each of you £1,200 better off. Joining the club means that you will never have to look back, but always forward, to wealth, fulfilment and happiness. It is necessary, however, for us to ensure that you are both fit to be members. Tonight we saw a little less of Sylvie than we wished, which is why Heidi joined in. We will require Sylvie to undergo a period of training. No harm will come to her and you will be re-united at the end of the training period. Meanwhile, you have promises to keep and Heidi will join you in ensuring that those are successfully undertaken."

"What do you mean, a training period? How long will we be apart?"

"Sylvie is a submissive, and a very beautiful one. She also has brains and apart from her sexual submissiveness she has a strong personality. It is our aim to work on her physically, mentally and emotionally to strengthen all three. She will, at the end, be more sexually submissive, have an even stronger and well defined personality and will improve in her ability to use her intelligence. Our training programme will guarantee to make her even more beautiful and physically strong."

"But Sarah, er, Sylvie isn't my property. I can't say whether she should undertake your training programme or not. It's up to her."

"We have already discussed this with her. We took her to her dressing room whilst you encountered Heidi's skills. She saw only the earliest sequences. Sylvie has agreed to be a trainee here, provided that you approve."

"I really don't know what to say."

"But you already knew that Sylvie enjoyed being beaten and was also an exhibitionist," Ivan interjected.

"You thought you might capitalise on a rare collection of talents, and so it has turned out," the Master reminded him. "In three months you could earn far more than you earned in a year, and you could have a lot more time to yourselves. After our training you will easily double your income, and then there are the rich and famous who may wish to be entertained by you and may become your patrons. I'd say you have ten money making years ahead of you and then you will be able to retire or give your minds to anything else you wish."

"It all sounds too good to be true."

"But it is true and you may wonder why the club should bother. That is in part because we wish to develop new talent, but it is also because many of our members are managing agents for other people, as Ivan and Tania are with you. We are concerned for their welfare and prosperity and also for the maintenance of the very highest standards of performance. We will do our very best for Sylvie, whilst Heidi will do her best for you, and there is no-one who could do it better."

Ivan looked keenly at Nick. "We shall need your answer within five minutes. You will be required not to see Sylvie during the training, apart from that and the presence of Heidi, your life will remain the same."

"Well, I suppose," Nick began, "if Sarah has agreed, then I shouldn't stand in her way. When does it all start?"

"Tonight."

"Oh. Well, can I at least say goodbye to her?"

"No, you may not."

At the same time, Sarah sat in her dressing room under the watchful eyes of Tania and Heidi. From them the story had been a little different. The advantages were as they had been spelled out to Nick, but the idea and its implementation had apparently been Nick's. Sarah felt alone and a little frightened. She did not understand how Nick had disposed of her to these people, but Tania was very reassuring and promised the changes that had already been made to Nick. Sarah had submitted to the proposal but was concerned that she would not see Nick for some time and wondered how he would deal with the promised performances they had arranged. No mention was made of Heidi's role.

Nick returned home with Ivan and Tania, whilst Sarah was shown into a beautiful bedroom suite where a silk night-dress lay on the bed and there was a basket of refreshments. She was very tired and ran herself a warm bath, had a little to eat and drink, tried the bedroom door to find it was locked, looked behind the heavy curtains to find windows with shutters on the outside and decided that she was at least safe from intrusions. Bathed and comforted she slid between the satin sheets, found the bedside light switch and was asleep in a matter of seconds.

The following morning Sarah was brought a light breakfast in bed and half an hour later, as she was coming out of the bathroom a middle aged woman appeared with several sets of clothes on hangers. They were all very ordinary outdoor clothes. Sarah chose some plain underwear, jeans and a cotton jumper. There was a knock on the door and a young man came in.

"It's time we went to the training camp. I will bring the clothes."

They walked down the corridor together. Sarah was about to ask him where the camp was, but realised that he would not tell her. Down a flight of stairs, into another corridor to be faced by a steel door which opened electrically. A large garage came into view. Sarah was shown to a limousine, the back door was opened for her and she stepped inside. It was not until they were well out of the garage that she realised that there was an opaque screen between herself and the driver and the windows were darkened to the extent that no-one could look in and she couldn't look out.

She wondered quite why there was so much of a cloak and dagger atmosphere, but since she was unable to do anything about it she picked out a magazine from the rack in front of her and began to read, or at least she looked at the pictures. Eventually the car came to a halt and Sarah found that they had entered another garage and she was being let out of the car and into a dimly lit passageway to meet an elderly, but upright man who enfolded her in his arms and kissed her on the cheek.

"It has been a long drive, you may wish to freshen up, Maria will show you."

Maria materialised at his elbow, smiled at Sarah and drew her into a passageway, opened a door and showed her into an elegantly furnished room with a door in the side wall.

"Bathroom," she said.

Sarah took the hint and made use of it. When she came out Maria was still there.

"I thought you might like to know the programme for the rest of the day. You will have a light lunch with Don Carlos-he's the one who greeted you. Then you will have a complete physical examination by Dr Blanc. I will be present throughout as your chaperone."

"Surely, there's no need..."

"A beautiful, naked young woman alone with a man for two hours could give rise to unfounded rumours, or even complaints. With me there all that is avoided."

"I suppose there's sense in that."

"Then you have a computer based lesson on logic to contend with. Followed by tea and a rest and then, this evening, you meet the members."

"Who are they?"

"Oh they all have names, I have no doubt, but here they have names which are given to them. I've no idea what they do apart from come here, or who they are. But they tip very well indeed and they arrive in the poshest of hire cars. Just take it easy here for a bit and I will be back to collect you."

The day went on just as Maria had told her. The medical was a top of the head to the bottom of the feet affair with plenty of attention to blood pressure and pulse rate, together with rates before and after exercise and recovery times. Her most intimate parts were probed and examined and after a glass of water she was able to prove that she was neither diabetic nor pregnant. She blew in a tube and her ears were examined. Dr Blanc showed about as much interest in her as a human being as he would have done a sheep, had he been a vet. Sarah concluded that Dr Blanc was probably gay.

She sat about in the room she had been allocated and at some indeterminate time later in the day she was collected by Maria and she couldn't help feeling that the walk down the corridor was like the prisoner's last steps to execution. No one spoke to her until Maria showed her into a small room occupied by two large men. One of them held out his hand.

"Give me your clothes."

Sarah hesitated and the other pointed at her. "That's not very clever. Strip, before we do it for you."

Sarah turned away from them and started to remove her jumper and jeans. She hesitated again and a large finger hooked into her knickers and gave a quick pull. She quickly shrugged out of her bra and stood with her arms folded.

"Good. We'll take you where you're going."

They grasped an arm each and more or less towed her along a corridor and into a space which had no more than the tiniest glow of illumination. She felt herself lifted up and her arms raised and caught against some sort of framework. Her legs were similarly treated and she was left hanging like a starfish.

How long this lasted she had no idea, but she heard shuffling noises and then a match was struck either side of her. The hall was suddenly illuminated by two candles and she was back at the beginning, looking out at a sea of faces and smelling the acrid scent of the candles.

*

Sarah brought her thoughts back to the present. Considering how exciting her experiences had been elsewhere, she didn't rate the recent session very highly, possibly because of the absence of Nick. It was more ritualistic than exhibitionist. She had been returned to her room and, as usual, locked in. She had asked for a CD player and some CDs. She was not surprised to find a personal CD player, a pile of varied CDs along the lines she had specified and several packets of batteries. Sarah relaxed, thought of Nick, wondered what the next day might bring and listened to a Nardini violin concerto played by Vengerov. There was no disturbance to her night's sleep. She awoke and visited the bathroom, taking time over examining herself in the long mirror and noticing that she seemed to be thinner and more muscular than when she last had a long look. Even her cheek bones seemed more prominent and she could not only see her ribs beneath her skin, but her hip bones jutted out for the first time. She raised her arms and flexed them and saw biceps and triceps. The muscles in her forearms showed as grooves beneath the skin and she was beginning to develop an abdomen with some concave curves and an unexpected central division where the muscles showed through. She was no longer the feminine, slightly soft creature she had been before she started out with Nick on this adventure. Her face was as perfectly beautiful as it had been before, her body was wonderful, but both were different. She seemed more physically poised and there was an unlooked for degree of confidence. She turned to see her side and looked round as far as she could to inspect her rear view. She ran her hand down her back, over her buttocks and down her thighs. There was strength there and her bottom had decreased in size, as had her breasts which remained solid and with no hint of a droop, revealing the nipples upstanding on the upper slope of each breast.

She didn't know whether to be pleased or dismayed by her new appearance. On balance she felt that she had worked very hard to achieve this new shape and that she was pleased with it. When she got out of here she was going to have to spend some money on new clothes.

Breakfast arrived and she ate the low calorie meal and drank the black coffee. She sat on the edge of the bed enveloped in a large white towel. She was intrigued by how comforting a towel was, used as a garment.

Some minutes later Maria opened the door and called for her.

"You've got a new tutor today," Maria told her.

"Who is that?"

"I don't know, I haven't seen her before, but she was polite at breakfast, so I expect she'll be all right with you."

They entered a room with no furniture at all, but a thick, soft mat which covered the floor and extended up the walls to waist height. Even the backs of the doors were padded.

There was the sound of footsteps behind her and a young woman appeared, dressed, as Sarah was, in a large towel.

"Good morning Sylvie," she said, quite briskly. "I'm Terry."

Sarah saw that she was a slender woman in her late twenties, with dark auburn hair done up in a plait. Terry was winding the plait round the back of her head and fixing it with some large hair grips.

"This is a new phase to your training here. In the afternoon we shall go for a pleasant walk in the grounds and I shall ask you to talk to me about the work of Durkheim. I suppose that you must have come across him in your studies?"

"Oh, yes, but I'm hardly an expert."

"I know very little, but I wish to know more, so you will have an opportunity to teach me."

"I'd like that."

"I am here this morning because we feel that you have toned your body enough to start to use it in ways that I hope you will find enjoyable and developmental."

Sarah remained silent.

"Please remove your towel. Yes, I see, yours is a very beautiful and strong body. Now we will each try a little massage oil." Terry removed her towel and stood facing Sarah who was taken by the slightness of Terry's body and the tiny, tip-tilted breasts, narrow waist and slender legs reaching to a bottom, each buttock of which could be cupped in one of Sarah's hands.

Terry handed Sarah a small bottle which she had been carrying.

"Do you find me revolting?"

"No one could find you anything but beautiful. You are exquisite from head to toe."

"You are too kind. Now, take some of the oil from

that bottle and massage it into my skin, all over."

Sarah started with Terry's back and spread the oil over her white skin. She reached Terry's bottom and hesitated for a moment, but Terry gave no sign and Sarah spread the sweet smelling liquid over and between her buttocks and down her thighs and calves.

Terry remained stationary so Sarah walked round her. She spread the oil over Terry's shoulders and down her chest. She became a little hesitant about touching the girl's breasts, but overcame her shyness and swiftly swept her palm over each of them, feeling the hard and surprisingly rough nipples against her hand. She continued below her breasts and down to her navel. Terry had set her legs a little apart and Sarah bent her head and swept rather more oil than was necessary over Terry's belly and across her now glistening crotch and down her thighs and calves.

Terry took back the bottle and looked at Sarah. "You've been exhibited and people have whipped you and humiliated you. I assume you enjoyed it?"

"Yes, most of it."

"I expect that your best experiences have been at the hands of men," Terry enquired.

"All my experiences have been with men."

"All of them? Do you do nothing for yourself?"

Sarah felt she was going to blush and thought that this was ridiculous, given what her experiences had been.

"Yes, of course, but I haven't needed to since Nick arrived, and then there were the shows."

"But each of us starts off pleasuring herself. We have to get experience and fulfil fantasies somehow. And then, it's not always second best. So a woman's hand has travelled over your breasts and squeezed your nipples and then has sunk between your thighs and has so easily found your special parts and has brought you to orgasm."

Sarah blinked, "Well, if you mean my hand, then yes."

"You had the chance to rub oil into my skin, but you were embarrassed by those very parts of me that we share and are not given to men. You didn't ask me what I would like, and I stood there hopefully, and your hand was deft and supple, but I was unmoved."

"I didn't know..."

"You didn't ask. But I will ask you. I am going to spread oil over every part of you. Would you care for me to give you some pleasure whilst I am doing it?"

Sarah hesitated.

"I see. If it was Nick, or Ivan or anyone of half a dozen not wonderfully adept men, you would have been flinging your arms round their necks and begging for it."

"Well, you see, I've never..."

"No, and you won't unless you make a start somewhere."

"But that assumes I want to."

"I can't believe that you would fail to try a harmless new experience which just might be enjoyable."

Sarah knew that Terry was right. What harm could come from such an encounter. It would most likely just reinforce her prejudices.

Terry had already poured some of the oil into her hand and was attending to Sarah's back. Sarah had found Nick's massaging attentions most agreeable, but this produced a whole new meaning of the word deft.

When she had finished Sarah's back, Terry turned her attention to Sarah's front and quickly arrived at Sarah's breasts which she gently kneaded and used her finger nails to pluck out the already upstanding nipples. With her right hand she continued to spread the oil, whilst with her left she pressed and gently tweaked Sarah's breasts.

"There, that's not as bad as the dentist, is it?" Terry enquired.

"You're very clever," Sarah replied.

"No, I'm not. I'm just applying a little of the know how I gained from myself and what I have learned from other women."

Terry stroked oil across Sarah's belly and then down her right leg and up the left one. At the top of the thigh she moved across Sarah's vulva and with a tiny pressure sprang her finger between Sarah's lips. In spite of herself Sarah opened her legs and Terry slipped three fingers against Sarah's clitoris which promptly responded to the touch. Sarah put her arms round Terry's back and stood with her eyes almost closed. Terry pressed herself against Sarah and she could feel the touch of Terry's rigid and rough nipples. Terry worked at Sarah's most delicate and responsive areas and probed to her G spot with unerring accuracy. Sarah stiffened and an agreeable dew began to gather at the lips of her vulva.

"There, I knew Mrs Clitoris couldn't be denied," said Terry and slowly withdrew her hand from between Sarah's thighs, kissing her very gently on the lips as she did so.

"Oh," cried Sarah, "you've stopped. I was just going to, I was going to..."

"You were going to come. Well done, but I didn't think I should reward someone who treated me so badly."

"I'm so sorry. I don't think I could be as clever as you at that."

"But you didn't even try. Now I'll tell you what this is about. You have to learn to wrestle. What is more you have to learn to wrestle, naked, with me. You will soon find that you no longer fear contact with a member of your own sex. You might just come to like it. We'll work through a practice session and then we will have a proper encounter.

This is a case of no holds barred, but in our case this means no biting, scratching or punching. Now, I'll show you."

Sarah had learned a good deal at Karate and Kick boxing, but she was unprepared for the swiftness with which Terry slid her oiled body against hers and showed her a fall.

"Getting your opponent down isn't much of a problem, it's what you do next which counts."

Sarah found herself on her back with Terry inflicting a scissors grip on her body with her legs. She struggled to get away, but the oil and Terry's speed of movement defeated her. Sarah tried the knees up and thrust to unseat Terry but she tightened her grip with her legs and seized one of Sarah's arms. This should have made things very difficult for Sarah, but she was able to wrench her opponent off her and she leaped to her feet. Terry's immediate response was to sweep Sarah's legs from under her and as she hit the floor to throw herself on top of Sarah catching an arm in each hand.

"The aim is to disable your opponent without letting

them do damage to you. A win is recorded by pinning your opponent to the ground so that both shoulders are touching the floor. In our sort of bouts, we usually set the number of wins a bit like tennis scoring with a maximum of say, five or ten and a difference of two once the limit is reached."

Terry lay on Sarah and held her down to a count of ten. Sarah, much to her chagrin, found that she had liked it.

They stood facing one another after the briefest of pauses, and this time Sarah made a quick rush on Terry, grasping one arm and swinging her round and forcing the arm up her back. Terry bent almost double as Sarah twisted and attempted a somersault over her own and Sarah's arm, but it didn't work. Sarah tried to catch Terry's other arm, but she soon realised that however slender Terry might be, she was also strong and lithe and the oil made it difficult to keep a firm grip. Sarah tried kicking Terry behind the knee to bring her down, but lost her own balance and they fell in a heap. Terry twisted in Sarah's grip and in an instant Sarah found herself with one leg pulled up by Terry's arm behind her knee whilst she was pinned down by Terry lying across her chest. The unusual feel of Terry's body against hers made her pause whilst Terry strengthened her grip.

Sarah would have known just what to do if this had been a naked man lying across her, but she was most unsure about what to get hold of to have any powerful effect. She was well aware that if she let Terry get on with it she was going to be in for a second defeat. She tried a headlock with her free arm but the slippery oil and the odd angle made this quite ineffective. She tried thrusting her raised leg down, but Terry had got it so far up that there was less opportunity for rapid purchase against Terry's side than there might have been. A sudden pain in her left breast made Sarah aware that Terry was biting her nipple. It was definitely time for action of some sort, and failing anything more technical she swung her free arm down and smacked Terry's bottom with her open hand. Clearly, Terry had not been expecting this manoeuvre and slipped her grip on Sarah's leg. Sarah at once shifted her trapped leg and brought it round to form a sharp scissor hold at Terry's waist.

Sarah found that she now had both hands free and she caught Terry in the headlock that she had failed in just before. Terry pulled at her arms and hands but Sarah made sure she kept her hands clenched. Terry was obviously feeling the pressure from Sarah's thighs and her arms. It was now that she might submit, but she had no intention of doing so. Sarah, weighing up the situation started to roll, taking Terry with her and turning Terry on to her back whilst she still had control of her body. Both women were sweating profusely, which, with the oil, made their bodies sticky and slippery.

Sarah was about to claim the victory when Terry's knees hit her in the small of the back and dislodged her. Such was the strength of the blow that Sarah found herself doing a complete somersault, landing on her hands and far spread knees. Before she had time to turn Terry was at her back and had seized one of Sarah's arms and was twisting it up behind her back. Sarah emitted a croak of surprise and pain and leaned back to sit on her heels. She was immediately aware that

Terry had grasped her left breast and was pulling at it in a none too friendly way. Sarah tried to remove the clawing fingers with her free hand, only to have her wrist caught in a tight grip and her arm suddenly wrenched behind her back to join her other arm. She tried to free her arms, but the result was that they were pulled even further back and then were pulled together with her hands quite close to the back of her neck. They were now so far under tension and disabled that Sarah could find no means to free them.

It was only when Sarah felt Terry's fingers on her breasts that she realised that Terry was holding both her arms with one hand. The other one was kneading and pressing Sarah's breasts and then the finger nails explored her nipples with a series of sharp tugs. Sarah could hear and feel Terry's breathing and was conscious of her nipples pressing against her back. In a moment, Sarah had decided to roll over to her right, but Terry's control of her arms and her weight on Sarah's back made this impossible. Sarah felt Terry's fingers on her belly and a sharp finger nail poking into her navel. She let out another burst of exhaled breath and Terry moved her fingers down to what was obviously her chosen goal. Sarah tried to wriggle, but was rewarded by a fierce tug on her arms. Terry's fingers reached round Sarah's hips and penetrated between Sarah's spread legs. She felt that she could never shake Terry off, and she concentrated on the sensations that Terry was inducing in her.

She began to feel the warm flush of an impending orgasm, but at the crucial moment Terry removed her hand and smacked Sarah across her side, leaving finger marks for good measure.

"There, that's for smacking me," Terry whispered in Sarah's ear. "Do I hear you submit?"

Sarah was well used to submission and enjoyed it. What did it matter if she lost out to Terry? There would be time at a future occasion to redress the balance. If she submitted Terry would surely put her fingers back and bring her off. She was wrong. Terry released her grip and sprang to her feet. Sarah brought her arms back to a more comfortable position and began to rub them to ease the pain.

Suddenly and with no warning, Terry darted at her and brought her down flat on her face. She sat on Sarah's bottom and took a firm grip on each of Sarah's arms. Sarah flailed her legs about but made no contact. Terry began to grind herself against her bottom and she had an image of Terry doing her best to rub her clitoris against her buttock. She broke Terry's grip on her right arm and brought it behind her to catch Terry's crotch. It was a good move and she realised that she had several fingers inside Terry and her thumb was pressing against Terry's clitoris. Terry was making all the running now with her body writhing against Sarah's clenched hand. She had started to make a sound half way between a sob and a gasp. Sarah could feel the muscles contract in Terry's belly and at once snatched her hand away. She thought that two could play at that game and rejoiced in Terry's howl of frustration.

"We're about equal now," Sarah said, "neither of us has got anywhere."

A surprisingly conciliatory Terry asked if she wanted to. "After all, we seem to have broken through the barriers which were impeding you when we first met."

Hesitantly, Sarah leaned forward slightly and

touched the fingers of her right hand against Terry's mound of Venus. Terry drew in a sharp little breath and leaned towards Sarah, turning her head to one side and displaying a perfect set of small white teeth. Sarah began to kiss her as she felt Terry's fingers stroking her slightly parted labia and she began to press against Terry's vulva and instantly found her clitoris with her thumb.

Terry began to penetrate Sarah in her turn and found her clitoris and her G spot at virtually the same time. Sarah shuddered, but her lips were too busy with Terry's to make any but the most muffled sound. She continued to work on Terry with her fingers and thumb. She slipped her fingers out of her vagina and touched her little finger against Terry's anus. Terry stiffened and gave a little cry, but used her free hand to move Sarah back to her original target. Sarah put her arm round Terry and pulled her towards her. Terry used her free arm to clasp Sarah and they felt their breasts touch.

Sarah began to open Terry's mouth and slipped her tongue into it as Terry did the same to her. Their breathing had become more rapid and shallower and their pulse rates had increased markedly. Sarah pressed her fingers faster and faster into Terry as she felt the deeper and deeper penetration of Terry's fingers inside her own vagina, until it felt as if her whole hand was buried in Sarah's body. Terry began to sway and their breasts chafed against each other as they moved. They broke off their kiss and both looked down at what they were achieving between each other's thighs. The effects of their fingers, the kiss, their closeness, and the touch of each other's breasts was becoming apparent. Sarah had awoken Terry's clitoris so that it was showing between her lips. Sarah had opened her legs so far that she was grinding herself against her own heel as well as enjoying Terry's expert attentions. Both were dripping from between their legs, and now they were able to breathe more easily and make sounds they both gasped and as the pleasuring continued they moaned and uttered cries of delight. Sarah felt the contractions in her belly which came before an orgasm and devoted all her attention to Terry, in the hope that she could delay her climax and bring Terry to the point of no return.

Terry must have felt what was happening to Sarah, and was immediately stimulated to

her own climax. Their orgasms did not arrive at the same moment, but were sufficiently close to be in tune with one another. Neither let go of the other and their probing fingers and renewed body pressure and their passionate kiss became a package which continued well beyond the usual experience of orgasm. The two naked women clung to each other in joyous and bewildering ecstasy and kissed each other again and again.

Very slowly the fires within them were dampened and there came over them a peace and pleasure in each other's company and in each other's bodies which was quite new to Sarah. When words became appropriate she whispered to Terry.

"You've won me over. I didn't know that it could be like that. Now I'm frightened I might lose you."

"We'll be together now for the whole of your training, though I will not be doing all of it."

"And after that?" Sarah enquired.

"After that we'll have to see, but I'll do all that I can to stay in touch."

Sarah thought this was a bit cooler than she wished , but decided that if this was the beginning of their relationship, then making sure it matured would be her main aim. All at once she thought of Nick and realised that she would, indeed be quite a different person when she had completed her training. In the afternoon Sarah put on a tiered cotton dress and went to her class on symbolic logic and tried to fight off the insistent memories of the morning and her hopes for the future.

*

Nick had missed Sarah, but he had been forced by circumstances to co-operate with Heidi, whom he respected, even if he wasn't taken with her. Heidi turned up at Ivan and Tania's exactly at the time agreed and they went through their new routine. Tania was quick to remark that Heidi was not as submissive as Sarah and that her enjoyment of pain was probably as much in giving it as receiving it. Despite these differences Heidi was very organised and was a good actor so that only the most discerning would register that additional frisson of pleasure and the need to do exactly what her master required. Heidi had at least as much to give as to receive and didn't mind making sure that this was apparent. The lengthy session, edited by Tania and Ivan, at last concluded and it was time to go. It was apparent that Heidi had no transport. Nick asked her if he could give her a lift.

"Not unless you fancy driving to Aylesbury," she replied.

"Can I take you to a hotel? It's far too late to be going all that way."

"The simplest thing would be for me to go home with you. I'm sure I could curl up somewhere, and I have all the things I need for tomorrow, and the show, in my bag."

Nick could find no words to refuse and Heidi climbed into the car.

It was quite a short drive home, avoiding congestion charge areas and with a slot by the side door in which it was just possible to park, though a passenger would have to get out before this manoeuvre was attempted. They entered the house and Nick went to make a cup of tea. He introduced Heidi to the sofa, which fortunately had a longer seat than Heidi had height. He dug the spare duvet and its cover out of the linen chest and found a couple of pillows.

Heidi looked round the flat with apparent interest.

"Not much of Sarah's things here."

"Not really very much of either of our things. We concentrated on the furnishing and carpets. Neither of us likes a lot of nick-nacks."

"It's not just that. This place is very masculine."

"I'd never thought of it like that. I don't think of myself as particularly masculine."

Heidi snorted in disbelief.

"In any case Sarah had as much to do with the planning, choosing and installing as I did."

"But you have failed to take into account how clever she is, and the sort of submissive personality which she is. Submissives are also very good manipulators and she will have made sure that you have had your way so that she could satisfy her desire to be subservient."

"She's only submissive where sex and pain are concerned."

"You love her." It was more a statement than a question. "And yet you managed one hell of a hard-on at the club. I always thought that there had to be a good deal of attraction before a man could manage quite such a splendid erection. It wasn't the whipping which did that for you, because you didn't particularly enjoy it, I noticed."

Nick looked into his mug of tea and mumbled an indistinct reply, looking decidedly shifty.

"Never mind, you'll see plenty of me in the near future, but you will have to adapt to me as opposed to Sarah. We work quite differently."

"I'll do my best, and you certainly have all the equipment that is necessary."

Heidi deliberately misunderstood him, "And I'm quite tasty in my own way."

"That's the understatement of the year, and you know it."

"Thank you. You're not too bad yourself. Now it is time to sleep. I shall have a shower first."

Whether that was a signal for Nick to retire to the bedroom was not clear to him, but he did realise that he had omitted to provide towels for her and collected a couple and put them in the bathroom. As he turned from his errand he came face to face with Heidi who had removed and folded her clothes neatly and arranged the duvet to her satisfaction. Quite naked, she brushed past him and he felt again those stirrings that had let him down the first time that they had met. Could it be that any attractive, naked woman would have the same effect on him? He doubted it. What about

Sarah? Well, Sarah wasn't there and it was anybody's guess what she would be doing and enjoying where she was.

Heidi came out of the bathroom and wished him good night. Nick came to himself and went into his bedroom. From there it was a step to the bathroom and then a quick slide into bed. He picked up a book but the turgid prose soon had him nodding off. He remained awake just long enough to switch off the bedside light and fell into an uneasy doze.

It had been hard for him to adjust to having another person in his bed, but once he had adjusted to Sarah's presence he had almost taken the friendly body beside him for granted. Now the bed was empty and slightly chilly. He couldn't reach out and touch skin and he realised that this was just another part of missing Sarah.

He slept fitfully, but sank into a deeper sleep just before dawn. He came awake gently to discover Heidi's head on the pillow beside him, Heidi's arm across his side and Heidi's breasts pressing against his back. For a moment he began to feel outraged, but the quiet breathing of his companion, her friendly and unobtrusive contact soothed him and he turned over and slipped an arm beneath her neck and gently drew her to him. Heidi made a noise somewhere between a gasp and a purr and snuggled into his arm. Nick realised he was again aroused and Heidi's slender hand slipped between them and taking his rigid penis in its grip rubbed it against her vulva, until, in a sleepy moment she gave a little quiver and a sigh of pleasure as she made herself come. Nick felt deeply frustrated, but Heidi's sleeping words were. "You shall have your reward tonight."

That evening, after Nick had gone to work, leaving Heidi at home, they met before going to Ivan and Tania's studio.

"You crept into my bed last night," he accused.

"I was cold."

"I'm sorry, I'll dig out some blankets for next time."

"Next time will be tonight, Nick. We'll be late back, and in any case I like sharing your bed, which is more than I can say about most men, and I think you liked it a bit, too. If we're going to work together in such intimacy, then it seems only sensible to get as much out of the fact that we have been thrown together as we can."

"But Sarah...."

"Do you know what Sarah is doing?"

"No, do you?"

"Of course, I was a trainee at one stage. Now the Club owns me."

"The Club.....owns you. What Club, what do you mean, owns you?"

"Wasn't all this explained to you?"

"Well, I know they're all like-minded people. But I thought it was just a club."

"It is. But it has a motto: 'Pain convinces us we are alive.' They are dedicated to the receipt and infliction of pain. They are almost all endorphin junkies, and I'm no exception."

"What does that mean?"

"Runners run through the pain barrier. It is then that the endorphins kick in and they can do virtually anything, like accelerating during a marathon. That's a rather different scenario from the Club, since the runner has the free will to stop. The training is all about taking away the free will and providing experiences which are so fearsome that you might quail to think about them, let alone endure them."

"You mean worse than being hung up and whipped till the stars burst in your head?"

"Oh, much worse, much worse."

"Tell me."

"There isn't a lot of point in going into details because the treatment of each trainee is different."

"What happened to you?"

"I told you it was about change. Before I went to do my training I was more interested in women than men. They convinced me that this was not the way to go, and, as you are aware, their treatment worked."

"But how..."

"It was all a bit Pavlovian and accompanied by some pretty dreadful punishments for the wrong response. It was a re-programming exercise. And there was a final twist to make sure that the change stuck. They introduced me to a man who was beautiful, kind, sensitive, considerate, appreciative, interesting, stimulating, knowledgeable, and the most wonderful lover anyone could have found. But he was gay and seventy five years old."

"But you said he was a wonderful lover. He's out on two counts."

"Not so. At seventy five he seemed to have attained wisdom as well as knowledge. I had wonderful orgasms at his hands. But one day he looked into my eyes and said: "Now is the time for parting and for you to make much of your new freedom. I have asked my grandson to visit you and bring you tidings of delight." He turned away, went through a door which was shut behind him and I never saw him again." Heidi looked past Nick into the distance and her eyes became moist.

"What happened then?"

"Oh, I waited an hour or so and then there was a knock at the door and a strapping and handsome young man stood there. 'I was promised to you, and here I am,' he said, I reached out a hand and drew him into the room. I tore at his clothes and he removed mine. There was no finesse, hardly any foreplay, but really, none was necessary. We thrust our bodies together and he penetrated me so long and so hard that the pain and the pleasure were mixed so that they have always remained harmonised in my mind and in my emotions. Later he whipped me as I stood in the centre of the room and I bathed in the delight of the sharp cuts he inflicted on me. I'm not like Sarah, I can't have an orgasm just from the whipping, but I do love it and it sets the scene for me to climax. Now, think what is happening to Sarah. When you see her again she will be changed because of her training. You will be changed because of me, better than that, you will be changed because of us. You will still love her, and she you, but it will be altogether different, and perhaps everything will change for both of you."

Nick bent forward and kissed her. She gave a great sigh, looked at the mantelpiece clock and told Nick that it was time to go.

Ivan and Tania had suggested that their act should be a foursome and Heidi and Nick had agreed. Tanya had choreographed the whole event and they had rehearsed it to ensure that things went according to plan. The men were to be dressed in thin lycra tights, and the women in short, loosely tied muslin tops and delicate embroidered thongs. They had taken with them a variety of items.

According to Ivan and Tania this was a venue which they had not been to before. It was a rather more complicated drive than they had bargained for and they eventually found themselves on the outskirts of a small town. The building they were looking for was the only one in the road, looked like a warehouse, and had a high perimeter fence topped with razor wire and steel entry gates. There was no one at the gates, but Ivan produced a credit card sized piece of plastic from his pocket and inserted it in a slot in a none too visible box. At once the doors opened and they drove through. As soon as the car was clear of the gates they closed with a loud clang and a draw bar completed the security arrangements.

"Not anxious for unexpected visitors," Nick remarked, "and difficult to get out if you're in a hurry."

Ivan grunted his agreement and wondered aloud where the entrance was. Almost at once a series of small lights at about car bumper height, glowed to the right of where they were. Tania pointed them out and Ivan drove slowly alongside them. They promptly disappeared, but this was because they had reached the end of the building and needed to turn left to follow the side wall. A new band of lights appeared and these, too, disappeared as they reached the end of the wall and turned left. There were no lights here and the space before them was pitch dark. They must have crossed a sensor as a very powerful overhead light on a twenty five metre tower illuminated the back of the building. There was a sign to the car park and Ivan chose a space in what seemed a totally empty park nearest to what appeared to be the closed front entrance.

Tania told them all to stay in the car whilst she investigated. She slipped out of the car and walked over to the door. This was a heavy steel roller shutter. As she approached it a voice indicated that there was an intercom to the right of the door and that identification was required. Tania spoke into the intercom and indicated who she was and what they were there for. The voice told her that the door would be opened in three minutes' time and that they would have ten seconds to enter.

Tania trotted back to the car to relay the message, but they had already heard it and were collecting everything that they needed from the car. They stood by the door which eventually rose about two metres and then stopped. As soon as all four of them were inside, the door slammed down behind them and a light came on. Nick could see the CCTV cameras watching them. After a minute a second door opened and they walked into the foyer of what looked like an upper class hotel. There was a young man behind a desk who greeted them politely then pressed a button on the desk and three heavily built, uniformed men appeared.

"Take all these bags and equipment to the dressing rooms." There was no word from the trio, but everything vanished down a corridor.

"Where is everyone?" Heidi asked.

"They're all here," the receptionist replied.

"But the car park's empty apart from our car."

"That's the visitors' car park," she was told, "and some of the members park on the roof."

"On the roof....?" Heidi said.

"Helicopters," Nick informed her.

"We don't know our way around here," Tania told the receptionist.

"The first thing is to ensure your personal security. All internal door are operated by palm recognition. There's a box on the right of each door. You just put your palm flat against the glass. But first we'll have to enter you into the system."

Each of them placed a hand on a panel on the desk which had a light which winked at them.

"That's OK then. I'll get a porter to show you where to go."

A tall, dark haired young woman appeared and stood about three metres from them. She was dressed in what they would shortly discover was the uniform worn by women servants in the establishment. It was as well that the building was well heated, because the black leather harness which was worn at the upper part of the body and the leather thong were not designed for warmth. A pair of glittering high heeled shoes completed the costume.

"Good evening, sir, and ladies and gentlemen," she said in a slightly husky voice.

"Right, Twenty two will show you the way. If there is anything you want just open your door and tell Twenty two. It's her responsibility to look after you."

"Please follow me," Twenty two asked them and they did just as she asked, all four being fascinated by the chain which dangled from her harness and fell between her buttocks with a gold number twenty two on it. She had the gait of a catwalk model, putting each foot down carefully and tilting her hips rhythmically as she did so. Nick couldn't make up his mind if this was a carefully rehearsed seduction or whether she was just lucky enough to walk like that.

Doors were opened for them by Twenty two placing her palm on the recognition screen. After the second one Tania asked if she could try and was relieved to find that her palm was recognised. They arrived at a door with a star on it. Twenty two stood aside and invited Heidi to open it. Heidi was also relieved to find that her palm was recognised. The door opened and Twenty two invited them to walk in. Everything that they had brought with them was arranged neatly to one side of a large room which had an open doorway to another, similar sized room. There were two bath rooms, make up desks, sofas and chairs and doorless wardrobes for their clothes. Twenty two was about to go, but Heidi stopped her.

"Where will you be?" she asked.

"I will wait in the corridor."

"No you won't," Heidi told her, "you will stay with us in here so that we can get your help at once."

"Very well, madam."

"Less of the madam," Heidi started to say, but Twenty two cut her short.

"We are not permitted to know or use names, madam."

"I've never met a place with quite such amazing security," Ivan commented.

"We have a very select clientele," Twenty two told him.

"Now, let's see. I think we've about an hour before we're due to perform," said Tania. "I suggest that we put on our costumes and have a final run through, we can use the other room. What's the performance area like, Twenty two?"

"I am permitted to show just one person and the other three must not go out of the door."

"Alright. Anyone else fancy going?"

They agreed that she should go and report back. It was very little distance to a large room with heavily padded chairs ranged in a horse shoe shape.

"You will work right up to the audience," Tania was told, "and you mustn't mind if some of them are keen to join in."

"I don't fancy that a lot," Tania replied.

"There is nothing you can do about it, I'm afraid," Twenty two told her. "But there will be twelve stewards present who will make sure that you are safe and that no one gets hurt unless they wish to be."

Tania was thoughtful, but slightly relieved by the presence of the stewards. She suspected that she had already met three of them and knew that all four of them, fit as they were, wouldn't want to take on one of them.

"What about lighting?" Tania asked.

"I'll show you," Twenty two said, and went over to a console. "You will enter in complete darkness. I will lead you in. I will stop you and then withdraw to behind the chairs. The lights will be worked by the lighting technician. He does a remarkably good job, considering he never sees a rehearsal. He also supplies the music, but this is wall paper rather than an ingredient of the drama. May I ask you a question, please?

"Of course."

"Does your show involve a lot of pain?"

"A fair amount, but we know what we're doing and we're very experienced."

"Oh," Twenty two looked somewhat dismayed.

"What's the matter?" Tania asked her.

"Well, you see, if the guests like you a lot, some of them will try to copy your act and if there is pain to be inflicted then we are the ones who are on the receiving end, and they are not skilful or experienced."

"That's really very bad. Can't we intervene?"

"Not beyond your act. You will be gone by the time it gets rough. We are slaves, you see."

"Slaves?" Tania was aghast.

"To all intents and purposes, though they are usually kind to us and when it is time for us to finish here, we receive our wages for the time we have been here and a substantial bonus which helps to set us up outside."

"How long are people here?"

"It's usually between one and three years. Leaving has nothing to do with us losing our looks, it's just that the guests get tired of the same faces and the same bodies."

"How long have you been here?"

"Just over two years. Part of me wants to go, part of me is frightened to face the outside world."

"Did you know what you were letting yourself in for?"

"Not really."

"Why doesn't one of you complain to the police when they become free."

"Needless to say we have to sign a fidelity and confidentiality contract. But it's really because we want to go on living and we're well aware that anything which blew the gaffe would mean that none of us was ever seen again."

"Wow."

They returned to the dressing room and Tania told

the others about the space and the lighting and music and how they would make their entry. She carefully omitted any reference to the powers of the owners or the possible fate of Twenty two and her companions. Tania put on her costume and they started a carefully edited version of the act. Tania timed it at thirty seven minutes.

"Is that likely to be enough?" Ivan asked.

"Yes, I think so, in any case there are other entertainments available both before you and after, and the guests won't want to wait too long before they become interactive."

Tania told the others about the possibility of some of the audience joining in. Both Ivan and Nick looked concerned. Heidi laughed, "If they want to find out what it is like I suggest we strip them and give them a damn good hiding."

"What if there are several?" Nick asked.

"The stewards will ensure that there are never more than two," Twenty two told him, "and in any case stripping them won't be difficult. According to that clock we have less than five minutes before you are to go on. Anything I can help you with?"

"No, but thanks very much for your help," Tania said and there was agreement from all of them.

They waited outside the door of the room which Tania had already visited. There was laughter and a rattle of glasses. Twenty two opened the door a fraction and light spilled out into the dark corridor. She grasped Heidi's hand.

"Hold hands," she whispered.

Suddenly there was utter darkness and Twenty two opened the door and led them in. They took about twelve steps and stopped. Twenty two whispered, "Stand still," and drifted away, presumably very confident of her ability to find her way in the impenetrable blackness. The four moved closer to one another and were suddenly caught in a powerful spotlight. There was a polite round of clapping and the light began to dim and side lights lit them in a warm glow, whilst music with a heavy beat began as an introduction to their show. The two couples moved apart to stand at what seemed to be the four corners of an undrawn square. Tania and Nick took a step forward and then engaged one another with whips. Tania proved remarkably good at fending off Nick's blows, but he caught her with a slash to her side as she returned the blow, but to his chest. They grunted at the immediate pain, but continued to engage one another fiercely. After a couple of minutes of largely successfully parried blows Nick caught Tania across her back with a full power slash. Tania visibly reeled and Nick took advantage of the situation to cut her across the belly followed up with an awkward slash to the buttocks. Tania dropped her whip and as she bent for it Nick caught her twice across the back. Tania uttered a distressed cry and Ivan entered the melee and caught Nick a hard cut across the back of his thighs. Ivan appeared not to have noticed that Heidi had also joined in, and after she had aimed a blow at Tania, which caught her across her belly, she turned her attention to Ivan and slashed him three times before Tania had her revenge, lashing Heidi back and front. Meanwhile Ivan was engaged with Nick and neither of them seemed to have much advantage, though they were increasingly breaking through the other's guard, as were Tania and

Heidi. In their case the whips had tangled in their all too flimsy garments which were beginning to shred.

The warfare continued with warriors getting in each other's way and everyone receiving occasional blows, some ricochets from a parrying whip, but others were getting through and causing pain and showing weals. Without warning there was a shout of "Stop!" from the audience and a large man stark naked came into the light. Judging by his slurred voice he was much the worse for drink.

"You," he commanded, pointing at Ivan, "give me that whip and shove off a bit. This is all a put up job. I'll show you how to do it, and how to take it."

The two women, now naked apart from tiny G strings looked rather apprehensive. The stranger announced that they were to be prepared to howl. He brandished the whip above his head and immediately received hefty cuts from all three of the performers. He let out a howl himself and swept his whip down and round like a scythe, only to have it parried by Nick. As the tails of the two whips intertwined, Tania caught him just below his crotch whist Heidi slashed at him from behind.

He quickly turned, and shortening his grip on the whip slashed at Tania, whose parry was less effective than it should have been and he caught her across the belly, making her double up for a moment. Though he followed up his advantage on Tania's back, he was quite unable to parry bitter blows from Nick and Heidi. Heidi caught him between the thighs as he turned and Nick striped him across the upper part of his back, burying the tail of his whip in his arm pit. His reaction was to bellow with rage and then start slashing ferociously at the three performers. They did their very best to parry his cuts but more than one got home and the recipient uttered an involuntary gasp. He seemed to want to disable Nick and take his fury out on the women, particularly Tania. He failed to notice Heidi, who was taking relatively little part in the performance until she delivered a quite devastating cut to Bob's crotch reduced him to a moaning, crouching victim. Heidi was about to follow up her advantage, but Tania warned her not to and two of the stewards removed the now disabled man.

"Serves him right," said someone in the audience and there was general agreement. Ivan looked out into the audience and asked "Shall we go on?" but before he had an answer a redheaded woman of about thirty, dressed in a low cut green sheath dress walked up to him and smiled into his face.

"It was good, as far as it went," she told him, "but I'd like to see one of the women stand up to me in an accumulator." Her request was greeted by a great deal of supporting applause.

Ivan looked at Heidi and Tania, both of whom had already undergone a good deal of punishment. Despite this they both nodded.

"The rules are simple," Ivan told her, "no blows to the face, otherwise nothing is off limits. Five sets and for the first four the receiver stands on tip toe and holds her hands behind her head moving round a quarter turn every time the drum sounds. There's no limit on the time between strikes, but at the end of each set the changeover is immediate. If there is a change to the pose then the woman with the whip at once gives up to ten strikes and is declared winner. The last set, the receiver stands with legs apart. If the receiver can stand no more she must lie down before the striker and lick her feet. Any questions?"

"Are those G strings necessary?"

"No. You have the right to ask for it to be removed at any time that suits you. However, you will have to remove your dress." Hooting and cat calls greeted this request. But the

redhead was in no way abashed, and after undoing a clip she stepped out of her dress to reveal a splendidly athletic figure, only marred by shapely breasts which would have slowed her down in any race. She had apparently not been wearing underwear and just a hint of copper fur outlined her crotch.

"I'll have the brunette," she announced, "and she can take off that G string right now."

Heidi complied with the request and the audience began supporting their fellow guest. "Come on Red," was the most frequent shout.

The whips were laid out in a line and Red was invited to have first choice. She weighed them in her hand and chose one with a buff coloured grip. Heidi chose an all black whip and cracked it for the benefit of the audience.

"I expect you'd like first strike," Ivan suggested to Red, hoping that her arithmetic was not very good.

"Of course."

The music started again and the lighting changed to a muted spotlight which showed up Heidi's tense body perfectly and allowed Red to move in and out of the shadows.

She waited until Heidi was sideways on to her and swung the whip across her belly. This was not at all like the warm up that performers allowed each other and a searing pain shot up and down from the point of contact. Heidi emitted a whoosh of breath and left her position and picked up her whip whilst Red adopted the pose. Heidi brought the whip across and caught Red just below the breasts. Red gave a loud grunt, but didn't move from the pose. The second blow caught her across the belly with a similar result.

The two women changed places and Heidi took up her stance. The first cut was across her shoulders, the second one fell across the tops of her thighs and the third hit her diaphragm and fiercely stung her right breast.

Heidi had the advantage of the extra stroke and caught Red just below the breasts and then two bitter cuts to the breasts immediately followed by another to the buttocks. She hoped that Red's endorphins hadn't kicked in yet and readied herself for the onslaught.

The five cuts were breathtakingly painful and were all delivered very quickly together giving her no time to recover from the first before the second landed. She realised that she had gone through the pain barrier and revelled in the euphoria they brought. As she waited for Red to take up her place she decided to go slowly, so that there was less chance of her getting the same relief as she was enjoying.

Red took the blows with her eyes and mouth wide open and her pelvis thrust forward. She uttered a brief groan as each blow landed and shook from her knees upwards.

It was now becoming a test of endurance and Heidi, having felt the bitterness of Red's previous onslaughts, prepared herself for the next attack with some premonitions.

Red went into the same routine as before, and Heidi could hear herself emitting an almost continuous howl whilst her belly, breasts and thighs were thrashed unmercifully. Suddenly she felt a small warm sensation between her legs and realised that Red had, by some unexpected magic, brought her close to orgasm.

Heidi ignored the shining patches on her thighs, but looked hard at Red, whose nipples were bright red with the blows they had received, and whose thighs, wonder of wonders, were showing the same gleams as her own.

Heidi cut her across the belly. Red bent back even further pushing her pelvis forward and exhibiting her cunt. In this position Heidi tried a cut by which the tip of the whip would catch Red's vulva. After all she had five more to get it right. Her aim was perfect and suddenly, Red's labia parted and her clitoris shone in the sharp light. The audience were entranced and Heidi let Red do a complete circuit before she struck her again just above the open lips. Red let out a howl and began to shake. Heidi followed up her earlier successes with three sharp cuts in the same area and Red began her orgasm with a vengeance, juice pouring out of her and streaming down her legs whilst she howled and writhed uncontrollably. She fell to her knees and took her breasts in her hands, kneading them cruelly. Heidi stood back. The audience were roaring their approval of the outcome. Red dipped her fingers in her crotch and worked on herself again, until she sat back on her heels with her knees opened far apart and pressed her fingers mercilessly into herself and pulled at her nipples with her free hand. Her head fell back, she uttered a shriek and the second of her climaxes tore at her body and showed every tense and straining muscle.

Ivan whispered to Heidi that Red was now hers. Heidi shook her head and whispered to Ivan. Red began to collect herself and Heidi helped her up. They clung together whilst the audience was delighted with the mutual pressure of their breasts and their bellies.

"Ladies and gentlemen," Ivan announced, "we are hoping that you will allow a small change in the rules."

"No, go on, whip her, now you've the chance...." came from the audience, but there were as many who wanted to know what was to happen.

"I am here for your amusement, and I won't disappoint you." Heidi turned back to the waiting group and gave Red her whip. Heidi came towards her and the two women embraced each other again and joined their lips in a long, deep kiss.

Tania and the two men moved to one side of the performance area as Heidi stood in the centre of the spotlight and raised her hands behind her head, standing with her feet apart. She raised herself on her tip toes and for a few seconds everyone had an uninterrupted view of her beautiful body stretched out to receive the punishment that she had not earned. Red measured the distance between her and Heidi and swung the whip until it caught Heidi a vicious cut across the belly. This turn of events was greeted with much approval by the audience. A second slash caught Heidi across her breasts and she groaned loudly. The third came up from the floor and struck her between the thighs and Heidi howled. The howl was cut short by the fourth and fifth cuts which struck home at her tortured cunt. Heidi was facing the audience, quite unable to move. A slow handclap greeted the long pause before the sixth, seventh and eighth cuts which produced weals across her belly, her thighs and her breasts. Heidi was beginning to wobble. The ninth cut hit her buttocks and Heidi pushed out her pelvis to lessen the pain. The tenth was a devastating slash between her legs and caught her sex lips and her clitoris. Heidi screamed and began to sag at the knees, but Nick and Ivan sprang forward and caught an arm each pulling her up to the vertical whilst Red hid behind her and seized Heidi's left breast in her left hand, whilst her right arm encircled Heidi's waist..

Heidi's chest was rising and falling rapidly with fast, shallow breathing, whilst Red stoked the fire of her passion and pressed both her nipples with the fingers of one hand. She slid her left hand down Heidi's body and inserted the knuckle of her thumb in Heidi's navel. After a moment when Heidi seemed to have stopped breathing, Red returned her attentions to Heidi's breasts. Red could feel the juice gathering at Heidi's crotch and knew that she was approaching orgasm. Heidi began to twist and turn and shook her head from side to side until she could stand the stimulation no longer and screamed her way into an ecstatic orgasm. Only the supporting arms of the three of them kept her from collapsing on to the floor and the applause from the audience echoed her shrieks.

The light dimmed, the performers who could, bowed to the audience, and the naked man from earlier on entered the performance area and took hold of Red. She put her arms round his neck and he swiftly put an arm under her bottom and lifted her up until she was astride his waist. The attention of the audience had shifted and Twenty two beckoned to them to go out. Nick was keen to see what would happen next and glanced back to see Red engage with the man to the full depth of his magnificent erection and then begin to lean back whilst he held her wrists with his free hand. Whatever applause the performers had received was eclipsed by the tumult which accompanied Red leaning back far enough to touch the floor with her hair.

The quartet took their time showering. Most of the weals were already beginning to fade, but some still left livid stripes, especially on Heidi's body. They dressed and collected up their belongings. As Twenty Two opened the dressing room door they could hear the sounds of a riot from where they had been half an hour before. Nick remarked on it to Twenty Two.

"No, it's not a riot, more an orgy, and I must see you out and return or they will think I am not as committed as I ought to be."

"I thought I recognised some of the people in the audience," Heidi remarked.

"No you didn't, and if you did you must keep your mouth shut and forget what you thought you saw," Twenty Two advised her.

They parted at the car park and wished Twenty Two good luck with whatever awaited her on her return. Ivan drove towards the gate and looked in vain for the card box. The gate opened and he drove through it at speed. After a mile Nick said he was glad to be out of the place and all three agreed. The car became warmer and Nick moved across the split bench seat to Heidi and put his arm round her, kissing her gently on her ear.

"You've had a hard time tonight, are you all right?" he asked her.

"It didn't go quite as I thought it might at the end and she hurt me a lot. I wanted to escape, but I couldn't because of you and Ivan."

"Oh, I'm sorry. We should have let you go."

"No, I enjoyed the beating and I enjoyed the touch of her fingers and I enjoyed coming, but somehow I needed something else."

"What was that?"

"I think it was you. Kiss me again." Nick did as he was asked and Heidi grasped his hand and pressed it against her breast. Nick at once felt a stirring and stiffening. He reached Heidi's hand to his crotch and she uttered a little mew of pleasure.

"The better part of an hour seeing me naked, and then, when I'm fully clothed, you seem to be pleased to see me."

"More than pleased," Nick replied, "absolutely desperate to get home and to bed."

Ivan took his hand from between Tania's thighs, where it had been working its own masterly magic and pointed to a London landmark.

"Home very soon," he told them, "and not a moment too soon. I didn't like that place at all. Some nasty characters there."

"How do you think they rated us?" Tania asked.

"An expensive warm up for their own acts, I reckon," Nick suggested.

"Probably about right." Tania agreed. "I reckon they've seen it all before and much more violent. It looked to me to be the sort of place where a bit of blood might be spilled."

*

Nick and Heidi held each other close and were pleased that they suddenly found themselves outside their front door. The four wished each other good night and Ivan handed Nick the usual opened envelope.

Once inside, little more was to be done other than a visit to the bathroom and then they fell into bed together. Nick found Heidi's head on his shoulder and her hand holding him. He immediately responded and she made a little whimper of delight.

"Lay me on my back, kiss me long and slowly, then penetrate me even more slowly and stay in me as long as you can."

Nick did exactly what was asked and Heidi reached up her arms round his neck and offered herself totally to him. He rested his weight on his knees between her legs and on his fore arms. He could feel her pelvic muscles pressing against him as he very slowly drew out of her and as slowly penetrated her again. She was smiling into his face but her eyes were almost closed and he continued his slow movements with great deliberation, each inward movement starting with a nuzzling at the gates of her vulva. Despite her recent experiences and the absence of foreplay, Heidi seemed to be deriving great satisfaction from Nick's attentions and he felt her begin to move her hips slightly beneath him. Her mouth opened and he kissed her softly. Her tongue flickered against his lips and he thrust hard into her. He kissed her eyes and she shook her shoulders. After a moment she began to arch her back and Nick caught one buttock with his free hand. He tried to remain calm and thrust slower and slower, but he got no further than deeper and deeper. Heidi began to rub her crotch against him when he had withdrawn and she cried out, "Now, now, shove it in, please."

Nick was conscious that she was about to climax and this brought him the classic prostate cramps. They cried out together. After a few moments Nick felt himself wilting, and he rolled to his side of the bed. Heidi murmured something and turned on to her side. Nick curved his body round her and clasped her left breast in his hand. She made a contented sound and he realised that she was asleep just before, in his turn, he slipped into a dream.

*

Sarah sat in a comfortable armchair trying to read Ian Suttie's The Origins of Love and Hate. How much more sensible this was than Freud, she thought. And yet Suttie was a self confessed Freudian. She thought of the time when the book was written. Freud was still alive, but very ill, though he was to outlive the very much younger Suttie.

Sarah was sure that the commentaries on Masoch and de Sade would have much to say on her condition. She seemed to have gone from being a reasonably carefree young woman to being inveterately wedded to the pleasures of pain, to the desire to display herself to an appreciative audience, and to have so far neglected her modesty as to engage in passionate sex for the enjoyment of others. So far she had remained faithful to Nick apart from her contact with Terry.

She thought about Terry. It had been an unexpected and exquisite experience. She wondered what effect it would have on her relationship with Nick. But then, Terry couldn't penetrate her in the same way, though the skin contact was as agreeable and the lovemaking beautiful. Could she settle for a woman, she wondered.

Possibly, if it was Terry. But she already knew that this was a temporary arrangement, even though she realised that she was in love with Terry.

Would she be submissive with Terry? Curiously, she rather thought she might be. What about the pleasure of pain and the exhibitionism. She realised that she was missing both.

And she was missing Nick.

In the early evening Sarah was involved with an hour learning classical Greek. As soon as the lesson was finished Terry called for her and, dressed in almost identical thin, flowered frocks, they went into the garden. Barefoot, they walked on the grass paths between beds of beautiful flowers and under arches of ancient yew which had been carved as hedges. There were signs that these had been trimmed recently and Sarah realised that she had no idea how this very large house was run, or who did the work, or who owned it, though she supposed that the Master had his name on the title deeds.

Terry engaged Sarah in conversation and they talked for some minutes until Sarah saw a wooden seat in a rose arbour and suggested that they sit down.

"Can I ask you about myself, Terry?"

"Of course, but I may not know the answer."

"What is the training for, and what happens next?"

"The training is packaged to meet the needs of each different person and so I can't tell you exactly what will come next, but be prepared for some experiences that are hardening for the body and the mind. I'll be with you to see that you are properly looked after."

"What did you experience which hardened you?"

"Several things. There was running and being

pursued by two men with goads to keep me going. That was terrifying, because I ran until I couldn't see and then I fell and they prodded me and stung me with the goads until I got to my feet and ran on. They chased me through a pine wood and the dead twigs lashed me and tore the few clothes I was wearing and scratched my skin. I ran until I thought that I had left them behind, but they were on me in a moment and the pain from their goads was excruciating. I ran on and realised that I could no longer feel anything and the world went black. I've no idea whether they prodded me again, though I had several unexplained round red marks on my body. They tied me to a tree and ripped off what remained of my clothes. From somewhere they produced litre bottles of water and forced them between my lips and made me drink. Then they sat across from me on a fallen log and watched. They told me I had to hold on to the water for an hour and a half and that if I didn't they'd beat me some more. It was a warm day, but the water had been chilled and I stood with my back to the rough bark with my arms tied behind me round the tree. I began to shiver and they just laughed. Then I felt the pressure on my bladder and at first I thought I would risk it, but then I realised that they never took their eyes off me and in any case I didn't want to pee in front of them. The time passed slowly and I was conscious of pins and needles in my hands and the need to piss was overwhelming. The men were whispering and then one of them got up and came towards me. He put his fingers into me and pressed half way between my navel and my crotch with his big, grubby thumb. I was distraught with the pain of retaining the water and the effect that his unwanted pleasuring was having. He bent and sucked my nipples and worked even harder between my legs and on my bladder. Despite the humiliation and pain and the threats I was becoming interested and I thought afterwards that there must have been something in the water because such savage interference would not have brought me anywhere near a climax. As it was I began to feel the pain and the pleasure mingle between my thighs and up my belly and I heard myself cry out and gain first one release and then the other. Water gushed from me and splashed over my legs and feet. I felt total humiliation at the same time as a powerful and prolonged orgasm and that experience made me associate flight and pain with the ultimate sexual pleasure."

"But what was the point?"

"The Master and his acolytes want to create as large a band of those who enjoy pain and connect it with pleasure as they can, so that they have a varied collection of people to call on for their amusement."

"You didn't mix the two before this experience?"

"I think I may have thought about it, but I rejected the idea because I didn't like being hurt."

"And do you now?"

"I can get a great thrill out of being hurt, provided it is ritualistically performed. What's more I also enjoy being abused and exhibited, something I would never have imagined before the training."

"I don't see what I am here for," Sarah said. "I think I already fulfilled the Master's specification before I started."

"But your first loyalty was to Nick."

"Well, it was, but things seem to have changed, particularly after this morning."

Terry leaned towards Sarah and kissed her, chastely, on the cheek.

"Then there's one change before you start."

"But I'm not sure that this will ever be a transferable skill. I was delighted with you. I doubt if anyone else could be the same, and I don't think I would want them to be."

"That's all very well, but this is an area which you will have to pursue. Let me ask you about Nick. Was he wonderful in every way before he found your fatal weakness?"

"I don't know about wonderful, but he was pretty damn good."

"And whilst you were with him you never thought about being with anyone else?"

"Well, there were passing fancies, but I didn't pursue them."

"Not at all?"

"There was one time we went to a party and I wore a dress which needed a ribbon across the bust, but we were in a hurry and I forgot about it so that a great deal of me was on show. Nick had gone to the bar and a chap asked me to dance and as I stood up he slipped a hand round my breast and gave it a quick squeeze, and stood back at once. It was a tremendous turn on and if he had suggested a walk in the garden I'd have followed him like a pet dog and hang the consequences."

"So, someone else might have seduced you away from Nick?"

"I suppose so, but it didn't happen."

"Though you might regret the missed opportunity?"

"I see what you mean. Something keeps telling me

to play the field a bit. Nick is my first serious boy friend."

"And you don't know if he's as good as you think, because you've nothing to compare him with. Now here we can arrange for you to meet the rough, the brutal, the expert and the ignorant.. What do you think?"

"I'd rather have another session like this morning."

"Don't worry, you will, but you have to have other experiences first, and as soon as possible."

Sarah swallowed hard and tried to get herself together. What she most wanted was to have Terry, but it seemed that this came at a price.

"I'll do what you tell me to do," she told Terry.

They got up and walked back to the house with their arms round each other's waists. Sarah loved the pressure of Terry's body, even through layers of clothing, and wondered what the following day would bring.

Sarah went to her room and had a long, hot shower, enjoying the sensation of rubbing the liquid soap into her skin and the powerful jets of water washing it off. She dried herself very carefully and used a good deal of skin lotion. She realised that she had not shaved her arm pits or crotch for several days and she filled the basin with water and soaped her arm pits and used the multi-blade razor with care. She rinsed herself and then dunked a thick face flannel in the hot water and applied it to her crotch. She stirred up a mass of shaving foam and brushed it, very agreeably, between her legs. This time she was even more careful and removed the slight, bristly fuzz which had developed and examined herself in the hand mirror, being very pleased with what she saw.

Sarah had asked for a dressing gown and one had been provided which was white cotton and was changed every day. She slipped into it, put her feet up on the bed and took out a novel of eighteenth century social life, which had been a considerable and not disagreeable surprise to her. She was reading a passage about a seduction in Vauxhall Gardens when she found that her unoccupied hand had fallen between her legs and was in imminent danger of adding to her pleasure in reading. At that point there was a knock on the door and when Sarah answered, Terry came in.

"You have a visitor," she whispered, "but he knows virtually nothing about women. It's your opportunity to teach him."

Terry went out and brought in with her a rather sheepish, hang dog sort of young man. Not bad looking, Sarah thought, but hardly a goer. He was dressed in a towelling dressing gown and slippers.

Sarah looked round for Terry, but she had gone.

"Who are you?"

"I'm Darrell, Miss, and I was told, er, they told me...."

Sarah couldn't bear to see the poor boy suffer. "Yes, I know, they told you that you could come to me and make love to me."

"Yes, Miss."

"Less of the 'Miss', my name's Sylvie, Darrell. Before we go any further, you had better have a look at me and tell me if you fancy me."

For the first time Darrell lifted his eyes from their gaze on the floor and looked at Sarah who had deftly drawn open the front of the dressing gown to reveal a good deal of her upper torso and most of her legs. Darrell didn't take long to utter his appreciation.

"You're gorgeous, Mi.. Sylvie." It was a sincere and wholly justified compliment.

Sylvie moved across the bed a bit and patted the duvet beside her. "You can sit here and we'll talk for a bit."

Darrell did as he was bid but managed to sit at a distance from Sylvie who thought that this was going to be very hard work, but that it was up to her to make the best of it. She gestured him to come closer and as he moved he managed to give her a fleeting glimpse of a quivering erection. At least that won't be a problem, Sarah thought, though I doubt if it will be a lengthy experience.

Sarah talked to him about the weather and asked if he had a girl friend. He shamefacedly admitted that he had.

"Never mind, Darrell, regard this as work, and I'll guide you through what you have to do." This might have been a complete turn off for many men, but Darrell seemed to be relieved. "I shall ask you to do things that please me. Not all women are the same, but most of us share a few areas of similarity. Now lie down and put your arm round my shoulders, and kiss me." A few minutes later Sarah came up for air and suggested that the kiss might be just a bit more gentle. Darrell kissed her again.

"You might find, next time, that it would be agreeable to put your hand inside my dressing gown and fondle my breasts." Darrell looked as if he were about to enter Nirvana

His idea of fondling left much to be desired, but Sarah quickly put him right and he began to get the idea.

She undid the belt of her dressing gown and let it fall open. Darrell was so transfixed by the sight before him that he did nothing, except open his mouth.

"Come on, Darrell, it's your turn." At this he started to fumble with the belt of his dressing gown, but seemed to take ages to get anywhere. Even when he managed to undo it he carefully trapped it between his knees. Sarah decided on direct action and slipped out of her dressing gown and threw it on the floor. Darrell looked aghast.

"What's the matter?" Sarah asked.

Darrell blushed scarlet. "I've got a hard...a hard.."

"You've got a hard on. So I should bloody well hope. Let's have a look."

Darrell shifted about and got rid of his dressing gown, but tried to cover his crotch with his hands.

"For heaven's sake get your hands out of the way."

Darrell looked away and removed his hands to reveal a quite respectable erection, but one which was beginning to wilt. Sarah decided on encouragement.

"Very nice, Darrell. You'll do a good job with that," Sarah told him, sitting up and spreading her knees. "You see that there?" she asked him. "What you've got to do is make me come and that is best achieved by rubbing me there."

Darrell reached across Sarah and took a breast in one hand and used the other to massage her vulva. Despite herself Sarah felt a little glow of interest developing and she reached forward to clasp Darrell's balls in her hand and then transferred her attention to his shaft which was quite flaccid. Under her expert ministrations it very rapidly stiffened. Darrell kept up the good work, but in a very short while he began to pant and a somewhat glazed look came into his eyes. Too late, Sarah realised that her activities were having more of an effect than she had bargained for and Darrell was groaning and calling out whilst hot jism spouted from his penis and onto her thigh. He promptly desisted from his task, just as Sarah was becoming definitely interested, and at once became limp.

"Who told you that you could stop?" Sarah enquired and Darrell pulled himself together and began to massage her clitoris again. It was Sarah's turn to pant a bit and to again return Darrell to full fighting condition. Several minutes passed, both of them were breathing heavily. Sarah was dripping into Darrell's hand.

That's about as good as it will get here, she thought, and decided to welcome Darrell into her. She lay back and opened her legs. He clambered between them and Sarah grasped his shaft and guided it towards her.

Once she had initial contact she used the head of his shaft to rub against her clitoris and managed a fair degree of interest.

"Push in, gently," she instructed him and she guided him into her. Sensing that there was not to be an immediate bucking of the hips and gasping, she told him to pull out and push in slowly which he did, several times, being gripped tightly by Sarah's muscles. He seemed to get the idea and began to move in and out with increasing vigour. She found this quite an agreeable sensation and was pleased with the length of time that he could keep going. Eventually, Darrell must have received the warning signs of an impending ejaculation and Sarah was again impressed by the vigour and strength of his penetrations which were hard and fast, slamming her down onto the bed and rasping at her clitoris as his hard shaft plunged into her to the hilt. Suddenly the role of teacher slipped from her and she became a woman lying under a man and being given a good seeing-to. Her breath caught in her throat as he plunged into her yet again and she felt herself begin to melt. She cried out and from somewhere Darrell found the strength to redouble his efforts, she heard their pelvises slap together a she bucked up hard under him and then the overdrive of orgasm hit her as he too cried out and spurted another load deep inside her this time.

"It was my first time," Darrell confessed breathlessly after a few minutes. "Thank you for the lesson. I hope we can practice together again sometime." Sarah thought that it was very unlikely and went for a shower feeling just a tinge of regret as she soaped her burning crotch while Darrell was escorted out by.

"You were very kind to him."

"You were watching?"

"Of course," Terry replied. "The job is shared between Maria and me."

"So I have to turn the light out to get any privacy?"

"Not much help, I'm afraid, there's an infrared camera as well."

"I can't see any cameras," Sarah replied.

"You're not supposed to. But don't take it hard. Maria likes you, and I, well, I think I might love you."

Sarah pulled Terry towards her and kissed her. "I'm besotted with you," she told her.

"Which means that you will soon get over me," Terry suggested.

"Not the way I feel."

"Could you stand another visitor?"

"Do I have to?" Sarah asked.

"Well like it or not there are three more to get through."

Sarah submitted. Maria came in and changed the bed clothes and Sarah, now in a dark red silk kimono, lay back and awaited her fate. She realised that she had no idea what the next man would be like, but hoped that it might be the expert.

Terry returned and thrust a grey haired, rather stringy man into the room. The lights were dimmed and Sarah only just saw an arm shoot out and catch her kimono, half lifting her off the bed and pulling the garment off her.

She suddenly found herself swung off the bed and held against this unknown man's body. It was all too evident that he was pleased to see her. He turned her in his arms and stepped out of the boxer shorts which were his only garment. Sarah felt teeth biting her neck, a hand kneading her breasts and another thrust between her legs. Not much in the way of finesse, but good as far as targets were concerned. He pulled at her nipples and cupped each breast separately in his hand. His other hand left her crotch and took a breast and lifted her until her feet were almost off the floor. Steadying her, he ran his left hand down her body from breast to crotch and sank his fingers into her.

Suddenly, she feared that this might be Mr Brutal, but so far at least he had not hurt her, though he had demonstrated substantial technique in disabling her and doing what he wanted. Not a word had been spoken by either of them, the only sound being grunts. Sarah considered that she would be happy to give into this man and do what he wanted, though he had given no indication of exactly what that might be.

He turned her towards him again and pressed down on her shoulders, forcing her to her knees. The hot, slightly sticky shaft was pressed into her face. Sarah opened her mouth, swallowed as much of it as she could and nodded her head rhythmically. Spittle began to run onto her chin and he twisted her arms up to force her head forward. After a fairly brief time, he picked her up again and dropped her onto the bed on her back so that her bottom rested on the edge and her legs dangled with her feet just touching the carpet. He stood between her legs and taking his shaft in one hand pressed its head against her clitoris and proceeded to jerk it up and down rubbing it against her whilst his left hand pressed down on her breasts. Sarah submitted and lay back to get as much enjoyment as she could out of the encounter. After a few moments a pink flush appeared across her chest and ascended to her neck. She felt hot and sticky between her thighs and the cramp of orgasm began. She prayed that he would continue until she had reached her climax and felt his pressing and rubbing become much fiercer. She couldn't resist the flow of pleasure at the stimulation and started to arch her back and gasp as the orgasm took hold. In the midst of it she was seized by the hips and the shaft was sunk deep into her, pubic bone pressing hard against pubic bone until she could feel nothing but her orgasm and she became aware that her partner in this silent and unloving encounter had turned his eyes up, opened his mouth and was spurting into her. As soon as he had finished he withdrew and walked over to the door which opened almost immediately and he left her, still without a word.

"Did you enjoy Mr Rough?" Terry asked.

"Well I came, so I suppose that I must have done. I didn't really take part, I just submitted, lay back and got what I could from it."

"Very wise. The rough ones can become the very rough ones if you aren't careful. Maria is waiting with yet another lot of bedclothes, so if you'll have a shower I'll ask her to do her bit at once."

By the time Sarah had showered and brushed her teeth, Maria had gone. She switched on the bedside light and got into bed. She thought about what had happened to her and wondered what it had proved. She tried to read, but found her attention wandering to the encounter with Terry which she was busily trying to relive. She switched off the bedside light and must have fallen into a doze because the next thing she knew was a wisp of hair falling across her face whilst she was kissed and a breast gently pressed against her back.

"Oh, Terry, it's you."

"Lie back, I'm here only to offer you company and comfort and perhaps by that make it easier for you to sleep."

"You're so kind," Sarah murmured and drifted off to sleep.

By the time she awoke, Terry had gone and she felt disappointed. She thought back over the events of the previous day. How wonderful Terry had been and how different the men had been. The one ignorant but enthusiastic, the other almost completely selfish, but then, perhaps not totally, his preparation was harsh, but effective. She almost wished that it had been a bit more rough so that she could have had the reassurance of submission. Sarah realised that she needed that added frisson of handing herself over to the will of another in order to get the most out of her experiences. If that will was to hurt her, apparently so much the better. She contemplated how she had ever got to this strange situation. What was it in her background that made her ache to be dominated and hurt. She realised that these were recurrent thoughts and that she had no idea how to come to a satisfactory conclusion about them. She shrugged and thought that probably it didn't matter all that much. If you like it, do it, was a sensible approach. But there was more than that. She had discovered that she was pretty much addicted to the pain and also the exhibitionism. A year ago she would have shrunk in horror at the suggestion that she could display herself as she had done, but it all seemed small beer now.

Then there was giving herself to those two men. How could she have agreed to such a degrading action? And Terry. She'd never been interested in a physical relationship with a woman, but Terry had lit fires in her that it would now be impossible to extinguish.

She wondered what Nick was doing and whether he was missing her. It struck her again, that she was quite different from the person with whom he had parted just a little while before. Would they be able to pick up the threads of their relationship? Would they even want to?

The door slid open and Maria greeted her. "Got someone special for you this morning," she said. Sarah looked quizzically at her. Someone else stood behind her. She turned and drew in a strongly built man of about forty. As he stepped over the threshold Maria shot the door closed with herself on the other side of it.

Sarah started to say "Good morning.." but was cut short by the impact of the man's body flattening her against the bed. A large hand was at her throat whilst another was ripping at her legs. A big solid knee forced itself between hers and she was all too conscious of the dangerous position she found herself in with breath entering her lungs with difficulty. She fought back punching and scratching and trying to use her legs on her assailant, but without much success, except that he withdrew his hand from her throat and grabbed both her wrists. He towed her up to the bed head and swiftly tied her wrists to each of the bed posts, lying heavily on her as he did so. Sarah tried to scream, but the big hand was back on her throat. She made gurgling noises which seemed to have no effect at all on her attacker. In an instant he was holding her hips and thrusting himself into her. There had been no preparation and Sarah was quite lacking in lubrication. She kicked her legs as much as she could to minimise the penetration, but this appeared to do nothing but rouse the man. He thrust deep into her and then pulled right out and then repeated the same process, making her cry out each time. Sarah was appalled at the fierceness of the attack and could do nothing to repel it. She was amazed when he suddenly reached up and freed her left wrist from the bond which held it. Perhaps it was all over now, she thought. But she was to be disappointed as he grabbed her free hand and spun her round in the bed and suddenly turned her over so that she was face down in the rucked up bed clothes. He gave her a vicious slap across the buttocks, and ignoring her twisted right arm, shoved her so that she lay with her top half on the bed, folded at the hips and with her legs dangling and her feet on the floor. Somehow he had managed to be standing between her thighs and she felt a sudden unhappy pressure of a hand on her arse and a big thumb penetrating her anus.

"Oh, no," she moaned but the only response was the removal of the thumb and the entry of what she took to be the man's cock. Sarah had a singularly tight sphincter and the piercing agony of the unlubricated penetration was accompanied by a grunt from the man. He held one wrist twisted up her back whilst his other hand gripped her right hip as he forced his way into her. Tears ran from Sarah's eyes onto the bed clothes and she moaned at this agonising violation. There seemed to be no stopping the piston pressures of the man's cock forcing its way into her, but her moans were cut short by a hand pressing the back of her head into the duvet so that almost all breath was cut off. Sarah began to panic and desperately tried to lift her head, but the twin pressures made sure that she had no chance to save herself and before the world became utterly black to her she felt the cock dig its way into her again.

Sarah became limp and unaware of the buggery or its conclusion. She lay across the bed and was dimly aware of Maria holding her in her arms. The first thing she noticed was the stench of the jism pouring from her anus and then the sharp pain from where she had been penetrated and the unpleasant twinges from her wrists where they had been tied and forced up her back. She opened her eyes to see Maria's solicitous face.

"It's all right, Sylvie," she said. "Do you think you can stand up, my dear?"

Sarah nodded and turned over slowly. Maria helped

her to her feet and Sarah clutched at herself.

"My bottom hurts." She looked at her arms and saw that there were rapidly forming bruises on her wrists and arms. She touched her sex lips which were bruised and painful.

"Who wanted me to be fucked like that?" she asked Maria, but all the reply she got was to be helped across the carpet to the bathroom. Maria propped the ravished Sarah against the wall of the shower cubicle and turned the water temperature dial to hot and opened the tap. Hot water gushed over her as Maria sprayed shower gel over her. Her knees seemed to have resumed their usual state and she managed to stand up in the shower whilst Maria soaped her and turned her this way and that to ensure that the was no remnant of the attacker left on her. Maria took the shower head off its hook and pressed it between Sarah's legs, tilting it up to warm and wash her vagina. The feeling was not at all unpleasant and Sarah held Maria's wrist when she showed signs of wanting to move on.

Maria lowered the temperature of the shower water and took Sarah out of the cubicle. She appeared to be slightly less in a state of shock than when she had been brought into the bathroom but she stood with her head down and her hands clenched in front of her. Maria began to dry her with warm towels and carefully patted dry every bit of Sarah's skin. She drew a chair to the side of the shower cubicle and reached in for the shower head. She turned it towards the back wall and at little more than a fast dribble removed the shower head.

"Bend over, Sarah, across my knees." Sarah did what she was told as if in a trance and presented her beautiful bottom to Maria. She felt the slightly chill feel what she took to be shower gel against her anus and then the pressure of something being pushed into her rectum. Sarah was beyond wondering what this was all about and far from able to object.

"I'm just going to trickle some water into you. When I say 'get up' just go and sit on the loo and you will be completely washed out internally. It'll make you feel wonderful."

'Oh,' thought Sarah, 'I'm going to have an en..' but in her pain and confusion the word escaped her and she concentrated on the sensations in her bowels. These were mainly of weight and spreading warmth. Nonetheless, she began to feel anxious that she might have an accident and managed to tell Maria of her concerns.

"You're going to be quite all right but I think it's time for you to get up." Maria discarded the shower pipe into the cubicle and Sarah gingerly began to rise from Maria's lap.

Maria stood up with her and guided her backwards.

"Oh dear!" Sarah exclaimed, "I think I'm going to have a spill."

"No you're not," Maria told her and lowered her on to the loo seat, turning quickly and exiting from the bathroom. There was a pause of five seconds and then Sarah felt her sphincter open involuntarily and there was a sudden gush and release of tension within her as her rectum gave up the watery contents of her bowels. The emptying seemed remarkably lengthy, but finally the relief and cleansing was over. Sarah dried herself with some loo paper and flushed the toilet, transferring herself to the bidet and enjoying the sensation of the warm spray giving her a final rinse.

Maria had been right, the pains she had felt below her waist had abated and she felt warm, and clean. She took a bath robe off the back of the door and put it on and carefully opened the door. She was amazed at the transformation of her room. There were three vases of beautiful flowers, the bed had been moved from its original position and had been completely stripped and the bedclothes replaced by new ones of a different colour with the duvet cover showing a floral William Morris design, echoed by new curtains. The floor rugs and the sofa had gone and had been replaced by a pair of beautiful Persian runners and a chaise longue. The bedside cabinets had been replaced by sets of drawers and the lights had been changed for shaded halogen lamps which were attached to the bed head.

"How on earth did you..." Sarah began, but the figure on the chaise longue was not Maria but Terry.

"Nothing much is a problem when you have the physical resources and several willing hands to help."

"Where is Maria?"

"She was rather damp, so she's gone to change her clothes. And how was your morning?"

Up to that point Sarah had felt encompassed by Maria's care, but suddenly the savagery and brutality of her attacker came back to her and she burst into tears. Terry was quick to hold her in her arms and comfort her.

"Never mind, Sylvie, there really isn't any harm done. You might be a bit sore, but that will pass during the course of the day."

"But why should it have happened to me in the first place?"

"You need to get to know all sorts of men," Terry

told her. "Now we'll have breakfast and then we'll have a walk in the gardens."

As if by telepathy breakfast was brought in on two trays and was put on the bedside cabinets. Terry and Sarah piled up the pillows and slipped their legs below the duvet. They ate grapefruit and individual packets of cereal with cream and sugar and poured themselves hot sweet coffee. They drank it slowly and had a second cup each. Finished with the breakfast things, Terry reached across to Sarah and put her arm across her shoulders.

"I think you should have half an hour's sleep and then dress and we'll go out."

Sarah happily moved across to Terry and she was comfortingly held in Terry's arms as she drifted into an agreeable doze. It seemed only a matter of moments before she felt Terry stirring and she awoke to her surroundings. The breakfast trays had gone and there were new clothes on the chaise longue.

Sarah picked up a flowing skirt of the thinnest Egyptian cotton and a long sleeved low cut blouse of muslin.

"They're nice, but where's the underwear?"

Terry laughed, "You should know by now!"

They walked in the gardens, but took a new direction. They approached a high thick hedge with a door in it. Terry opened it and Sarah followed her through. They were in an amphitheatre with seats round three quarters of the circle and a stage area lower than the seats.

Sarah looked round with wonder. "It's an open air theatre," she said.

"Yes, and you will be performing here in the not too distant future."

Sarah looked at the stage and stepped down the ranks of seats towards the performers' entrance. She walked through the overlapping ends of the hedge where there was a passageway to a substantial covered building, half sunk into the earth. One of the doors stood ajar and Sarah peered round the edge of it. In the gloom she saw props of every sort imaginable, and quite a few the use for which was quite unimaginable. Terry entered behind her and switched on the light to reveal an Aladdin's cave complete with changing rooms and showers.

She wandered between the neatly arranged ranks of equipment and asked what sort of performances were presented.

"What sort do you think?" Terry asked her.

"By the look of some of that equipment and the props, some pretty remarkable stuff."

"You're right. There's a performance scheduled for Thursday afternoon. You could be a member of the audience and then you could meet Mr Expert."

Sarah winced. "Oh God, not after this morning."

"I think he's just what you need. Tell you what, after this afternoon's workout I'll bring him to see you and you can have a talk. If you don't take to him, fine. But if you do then you could be top of the bill on Thursday."

"What, are you asking me to be fucked publicly, after what we have had together?"

"It's all part of the training. You never know, we might get to perform on the Saturday."

Sarah had a feeling that this suggestion was in some way very closely linked to her acceptance of the first meeting. She hesitantly agreed to Terry's plan.

Mr Expert turned out to be a slender, good looking,

evenly tanned, softly spoken man of indeterminate age. He shook Sarah's hand gently when he was introduced and leant towards her. Sarah detected a slight perfume of expensive after shave and admired his Gieves and Hawkes summer lightweight suit and the perfect whiteness of his Tyrrel shirt. His shoes were highly polished and his grey silk tie matched perfectly the pearl grey of his suit. His hand in hers was strong and dry with immaculate finger nails. Terry looked past him to Sarah and realised that she had taken in all these positive signs. Sarah and Mr Expert sat down on the settee and everything about Mr Expert's body language indicated his complete attention to what she was saying.

"It is a strange thing to be talking to you like this," he said, "but I need to know exactly what it is you like so that I can provide what you wish. I have no other function than to please you."

Their conversation was long and detailed. He asked many questions and received many replies, which, in the nature of things, were occasionally contradictory, which led him to tease out a consistent answer. They drank white tea and nibbled at Arrowroot biscuits. It might have been a discussion between a famous couturier and a client. Eventually, Mr Expert rose to his feet, took Sarah's hand in his and kissed it.

"I do hope that we shall meet again," he told her and she smiled into his face with an expression of complete agreement.

Terry had been sitting on the far side of the room, quietly observing the meeting whilst appearing to be reading Vogue. "Well?" she asked, after they were alone.

"Well, he's a bit gorgeous, but also a bit fancy. He certainly did his best to show an interest in me, and that's always flattering."

"And unusual," Terry added. "How do you think of him as a partner in a show?"

"I really don't know. He's not big like Nick, or frightening like Ivan, but he has a lot about him."

"Much more than you could ever guess," was Terry's enigmatic reply.

Monday became Tuesday and on Wednesday Terry brought Mr Expert to tea. Unexpectedly, he came straight to the point: "Shall we be meeting tomorrow afternoon?"

"I haven't thought about it," Sarah replied rather lamely.

"That's not quite true. Like me, you have thought of little else."

"You're right," Sarah replied, "and yes, I would like to meet you tomorrow."

"Good, I can promise you a very interesting time."

Suddenly, Sarah realised that this man had power and that he was prepared to use it. She shivered. Once again she appeared to have let herself in for something which she was unprepared for.

"What do I have to do?"

"Exactly what I tell you to. I'll see you behind the stage at two o'clock."

He bowed and was gone.

Sarah slept badly on Wednesday night, her dreams filled with indistinct but terrifying images which brought her awake clutching her breasts or with her hand between her thighs as if to ward off some predator.

Terry appeared at half past one and led her through

the garden to the back entrance to the store. She was met by three women dressed in blouses and jeans and wearing aprons.

They led her into a corner room and without speaking quickly removed all her clothes. Cuffs were fitted to her wrists and ankles. They twisted a hemp rope and drew it up between her thighs and across her hips so that it only slightly covered her vulva. Next they took thin sticky-back plastic cut in odd shapes and moulded it to her breasts. Over these rudiments of undergarments they hung a thin pale blue satin cloak, secured at the neck and falling in folds to her ankles. Sarah loved the touch of satin against her skin but felt uncomfortable with the plastic and the rope. Her hair was pulled into a pony tail with a band next to her head and then twisted round into a neat chignon secured with glittering hair pins. She was invited to view herself in a large mirror, but she thought she looked pretty ordinary, though that was not an opinion which seemed to be shared by the three women.

Lots of activity had been going on behind her in the stage entrance part of the shed but she had no idea what it was all about. It was coming up to two and Mr Expert arrived. He removed his coat to reveal a lithe, wonderfully muscular body covered by a pair of skin hugging black tights. He received a mask from one of the women and adjusted it over his eyes so that he peered out of the holes in it. Outside there was noise and clapping. He gestured to Sarah to come to see what was going on and they looked out at the stage area. Unknown to Sarah the performances had begun. There were three crosses set in the ground leaning forward. On the two side ones there were naked women tied by their wrists and hanging forward. On the centre one a woman with a lithe figure was tied to the cross by her ankles. Beside each hanging figure was a man with a whip in his hand . The whips were plied on the swinging bodies in turn so that the audience could enjoy each one separately. The women were playing their part magnificently and greeting each crack and slap of leather on their flesh with resounding screeches and yells. The centre figure tried to draw her body up so that her back, rather than her belly and breasts would be a target. Her reward was to have a heavy weight tied to her wrists so that she was stretched as well as inverted. The whipping went on for some minutes until the women fell almost silent. A shout from the audience, whose members appeared to be dressed like ancient Greeks, demanded further action. The two men from the side joined their companion in the centre and at once there was a positive hail of blows on the girl's body. She screamed for a few minutes, but after rolling her head about with her mouth open and her eyes staring she became still and silent. The three diverted their attention to the girl on the right whilst the women who Sarah had met released the girl and laid her on the ground where she stirred and moaned. The thrashing continued until the second girl became silent and her head drooped with her chin on her chest. They moved on to the third girl and repeated the exercise. This one was the toughest of the three and dozens of cutting hits struck her as she leaned her head back and howled in protest. Her thighs, belly and breasts were covered in weals and eventually she, too, fell silent with her body racked by the pain of the hanging crucifixion and the flogging.

At that point there were three bodies on the soft grass. The first was attempting to move her legs and the upper part of her body, but a man put his foot on her chest. The second had come round and was moaning but hardly moving, whilst the third was still lying spread eagled and immobile. One of the men turned to the audience and said something which Sarah didn't catch. Whatever it was three men got up and walked on to the stage to the applause of the audience. Two of them approached the last of the three girls, but the bigger of the two men deferred to the other and turned to the second girl. At once they knelt between the girls' legs and clasping their hips engaged their cocks with the bruised and tender cunts.. The two girls were too exhausted to do much more than accept the penetration and wait for the men to satisfy their lusts on them. The third man met with more resistance, despite the fact that the girl had been the most abused. She tried to close her legs and push at him with her knees and strike at him with her fists.

In a moment there were three men at her. Two of them rolled her over whilst the third produced a tawse and began to beat the girl all over her back and thighs whilst he shouted at her. Her yells and then screams began to subside and she received some sort of instruction whereupon she adopted a crouching position with her knees under her chest and her head down and buttocks raised. The man whom she had attempted to repulse knelt behind her and pulled her cheeks apart, stuck a long finger into her arse and as she drew her head up in response plunged his cock into her. She arched her back and emitted a violent scream which seemed to please her assailant. He withdrew almost completely and then plunged in again whilst the girl shrieked.

Sarah well knew that the first penetration was often painful, but she was surprised that the girl should react with quite such vigour. Then she saw that the man was wearing a cock ring just below his glans and that this appeared to be studded. His contact with the girl's tender flesh would be as devastating as she appeared to indicate it was. Luckily her screams seemed to gratify the man so much that after a dozen thrusts he roared and threw back his upper body as he slaked his desire within her. He stood up and turned away as she pressed her face to the grass, gasping and sobbing. Two of the women seized the girl by the wrists and dragged her away from the stage.

"What was all that about?" Sarah asked.

"Three little beauties who wanted to join for the money and perks and then wouldn't co-operate. This is all part of their being broken in."

"Will I have to be abused like that?"

"Oh no," he said reassuringly, and then added, "much worse."

He drew Sarah back from the view of the stage and put a long arm over her shoulder and held her close to him. It was a comforting gesture, but Sarah found it slightly threatening as he held her as if he owned her. Sarah pulled at the rope which was cutting into her, but it had been tied by experts and she had no idea how to loosen it or get it off. She turned round to see the three girls who had recently been so badly beaten. They were cowering together between two pieces of apparatus whilst one of the women dressers stood over them with a cane in her hand. Two of the girls were crouching and holding each other close whilst their tear stained faces were turned up to watch their jailer. The third was lying on her side with her knees drawn up to her chest and her hand covering her face. Sarah wanted to go and comfort them but she was suddenly propelled onto the stage by her partner.

"Walk slowly," he told her. "Keep your head up. Look at the audience."

Sarah did what she was told and advanced to the centre of the stage.

"Stand still! Now, very slowly bend down and pull up the hem of your dress. Now take it over your head and drop it behind you."

Sarah obeyed and stood, barefooted before the audience revealing her beautiful body to them. This was all easy so far, she thought. From some overhead gantry a rope descended with a hook on it. She was instructed to insert the hook in the rope which bound her hips and crotch. No sooner had she done so than she rose two metres into the air. The disposition of her weight left her hanging with arms and legs dangling and looking up into the sky. The rope from which she dangled started to swing backwards and forwards in a steadily increasing arc. She found herself swung over the audience who laughed and cheered. She attempted to pull herself up on to the rope and as she did so she noticed that the rope she was wearing was unravelling. She began to increase her efforts to take the weight off it and, at the very last moment, grasped the rope just above the hook as the unravelling was completed and she swung in a long slow arc over the audience and the stage. Sarah became frightened of not being able to hold on and tried to insert the hook into the rings on her cuffs. This meant some seconds of holding on with just one hand and she came within an ace of falling off and hitting the ground.

Having hooked a cuff ring, Sarah tried to hook her other wrist, but found herself hanging by one arm and unable to do more than swing over the stage and the audience. She realised that the swinging was slowing down and that the hook was descending. She was almost stationary when she came to rest among the audience. They at once took the opportunity to feel her body and one of the onlookers reached up to her breasts and encountered the plastic covers. With a wrench which made her gasp, first one and then the other were ripped off and the hand that had removed them was pressing her breasts whilst another hand was probing her cunt. Sarah shook and tried to kick and flail with her unfettered arm, but the weight of her body was making her shoulder seriously painful and she tried to reach up and connect both her wrists. This was more easily done when she was stationary, though it left her more vulnerable to those who were abusing her.

Without warning the hook rose in the air and she was transported to the stage and set down. She freed herself from the hook and stood facing her master.

"Kneel down and kiss my feet. Now turn round and approach the automaton." Because she had been instructed to face the audience when she entered the stage area she had failed to notice a grotesque representation of a naked man behind her. The figure was larger than life and was seated. From between its legs protruded a model of an erect cock. The tip seemed to be exuding some sort of sticky fluid which was slowly sliding down the shaft. Sarah looked at the contraption with fear.

"Sit on his lap, facing him"

Sarah mounted on to the figure's lap. At once its arms closed behind her.

"Put your arms round his neck and lift yourself onto his cock."

Sarah strained her muscles and managed to position herself so that the artificial penis was nuzzling at the gates of her sex. She could feel the sweat begin to run down her back from the effort of holding on.

"Let go of his neck."

Sarah hesitated because she was frightened of what this huge phallus would do to her. The automaton seemed to be programmed to deal with the uncooperative and reached its hands to her wrists and hauled them up above her head. Sarah quaked internally that the next move would be to drop her on to the rigid cock, but instead she was lowered slowly on to it. She felt the penetration and howled, as much in anticipation as because of the pain. Her own weight carried her down onto the shaft, which if huge was also very well lubricated. Eventually her legs were as wide as was possible across the creature's thighs.

At this point her wrists were held by only one plastic hand whilst the other arm encircled her waist. There was a pause of ten seconds and the automaton started to move up and down on the seat, thrusting even further into Sarah. Both the automaton's hands were now grasping Sarah just below the breasts and moving her up and down relentlessly. She tried pushing at the thing's chest, but to no effect. This was different from being violated by a man who would eventually have at least a temporary relief of his lust. Here there was no lust, but a merciless penetration which she realised might go on until the automaton's power source was exhausted and long after she was no longer able to feel anything. What she could feel was the pressure of the phallus against the walls of her vagina and intermittently against the neck of her womb. She was having trouble breathing and was reduced to leaning back against the strength of the automaton's hands.

Suddenly the motion stopped and she realised that the machine was turning her so that she faced the audience. She now had her back to the automaton, though she was as deeply impaled as before. A mechanical hand touched her left breast and two of its fingers sought out her nipple. She tried to twist away from it but its work on her was merciless. Sarah looked down and could see the fingers tugging at her nipple and the shape of the phallus within her slim belly. The motion began again and she realised that she could do nothing to resist it.

Penetration, pain and teased nipples would normally bring her to some sort of climax. But here there was no involvement or emotion and all she could do was attempt to ride it out whilst her tortured cunt was plundered by the machine and the audience waited to see what next would happen. They had not long to wait, but initially they could not understand the change in Sarah who suddenly writhed and screamed. Then they saw the streams of liquid issuing from between her legs where the automaton was filling her first with hot water and then with cold. Sarah began to collapse forward off the automaton's lap, only to realise that the shaft had been withdrawn and the arms were neither holding her nor preventing her from getting off. Ungracefully, she slid off the thing's lap and landed in an awkward heap on the grass. As she lay with limbs not answering to her needs she realised that she had not been much hurt, but that she would always want some sort of human contact if she were to derive satisfaction from her submissiveness. She hadn't long to wait.

Two women picked her up and got her legs working as they walked her to the back of the stage. There they clipped her wrists and ankles to the spokes of a large wheel. As soon as she was in place Mr Expert approached with a long whip in his hand. He stood off to one side and flicked out the whip and gave her a sharp cut across the ribs. This was familiar territory for Sarah who did no more than utter a brief gasp. The second cut was across the top of her thighs and though harder she managed to cope with it successfully. The third hit creased her breasts and produced a brief cry. Suddenly Sarah realised that the wheel was turning on an axle and the next cut from the whip caught her from the navel to the collarbone as she turned sideways on to the whip. She arrived at the upside down position and received a cut to her vulva that produced a little scream, but the turning wheel meant that she was almost horizontal again as the whip took her from between her breasts to her crotch. In a moment she was hanging the right way up and the whip cracked across her belly, causing her to draw in her breath and exhibit the full arch of her ribs and thrust out her breasts.

The thrashing continued unremittingly as the wheel turned and then Mr Expert approached her with the wheel stationary as she was hanging from her wrists. Sarah felt dizzy with the motion and concerned that the biting cuts she was receiving would leave permanent marks. Mr Expert hung the whip at his waist and produced a bottle, some of the contents of which he poured into his hand and then proceeded to rub into her bruised skin. At once Sarah felt a pleasing warmth and she moved her hips towards his hand as far as she could and he swept his fingers between her thighs and pressed them into her vagina. Sarah registered the pleasure of his fingers in her and a small dew formed at the lips of her vulva. She pushed herself further at the pleasuring hand which again probed her with sticky fingers. Sarah was almost ready to come when the hand was removed and the figure in front of her stepped back and to one side.

At first, Sarah was pleased with the warmth which was suffusing her body, but the warmth seemed to be turning to heat and then to a sensation of burning which afflicted every weal on her skin and made it stand out and glow bright pink. Most painful was the effect on her vulva and vagina which became engorged and swollen with the sex lips parted and her clitoris twice its normal size and feeling tender and burning.

The sensation became worse and worse until Sarah felt that a flame-thrower was being directed at her skin and she began to writhe in her bonds and utter almost unbroken howls. In a rare moment when she became aware of the audience she saw one of the men leaning forward in his seat and licking his lips, his hands busy between his legs. Sarah had no idea what to do with herself and she moved continuously, the muscles in her belly rolling as she drew in breath and expelled it and twisted as far as she could in an effort to dissipate the heat that was burning her. Her howls transformed into a series of "Oh!! Oh!!!" as the liquid which had been spread over her did its ferocious work. At last there came a slight relief and the women untied her legs. Sarah dangled from her wrists and twined her legs together and then drew them apart. The now slightly less excruciating heat made her want to offer herself to whoever would dampen her fires.

As if he could read her mind Mr Expert gestured to the women to release Sarah's wrists and stood in front of her to catch her tortured body in his arms and carried her to what appeared to be a large mattress covered in a black sheet with cushions at one end. He laid her so that she was sideways on to the audience and stepped across her naked body to lie beside her.

He smoothed her damp hair from her forehead with a gentle touch and turned her face until she was looking straight up. Pressing his body against her side he leaned across and kissed her face, starting at the forehead and working down across her eyes and then her lips which he touched with infinite tenderness and pressed his firm straight lips to her soft curved ones. His hand stroked her neck and touched the lower side of her breast, slowly moving up until her left breast was completely cupped in his hand. He gently squeezed her breast and lowered his lips to her nipple which he took between his teeth and pulled gently until it became erect and her breast became turgid. He let go of her nipple and moved his head so that his lips were close to her ear. Sarah could feel his warm breath tickling her ear, but was quite unprepared for his whisper: "You are utterly beautiful and I love you. Very shortly I shall try to bring you to an orgasm and then I shall penetrate you and make love to you, which will be the sweetest experience I have ever had."

Sarah forgot the tortures, the whipping and the burning pain and moved her head to kiss him. His tongue flicked out of his mouth and circled her open lips sending a convulsive shudder of delight down her body. His fingers continued working at her breast for a few moments whilst he slipped his unoccupied arm under her neck. She became aware that skilful fingers were spread over her crotch and that some of them had entered her vagina where a slight stickiness was developing. The fingers withdrew and she felt two or three of them gently stroking her clitoris. The arm round her shoulders drew her close to him and their lips met in a sweet soft kiss. Sarah's world became centred on the touch of his lips and the pressure between her thighs. She opened her legs, offering herself to him and the fingers continued their master strokes as she began to open her mouth and close her eyes, surrendering to her passion and pleasure.

She could see the stars bursting behind her eyes and gripped him with one hand whilst the other was clenched in a tight ball of fist. Her panting became louder and she began to lift her hips. For an instant his fingers left her clitoris and she arched her back in invitation for him to continue, as she let go of the position she realised that he had placed a cushion under her buttocks. The pleasuring of her clitoris instantly resumed and she turned her head backwards. He had removed his arm and the cushion and was now kissing her breasts alternately as she lay on her back with her legs apart. Sarah moved her hand to make more contact with him, but caught his leotard and reached down to contact the sharp erection which was ill concealed by the thin material. He pulled at the front flap of the leotard and it came away from the surrounding material. Out stood as fine an erect cock as any stimulated woman could want and she seized it in her hand, running her fingers up and down the shaft and pulling him towards her. Her juices had been dripping for perhaps a minute and she was desperate to have her orgasm with him kneeling between her thighs and pressed deep into her.

She was not to be disappointed and she felt the sharp end of his cock pressed against her open sex lips and then slowly pushed in to the full extent of its length. She reached up with both arms and pulled him down on to her and as chest met breast he whispered that she was the most exquisite creature in her passion and that he would now enter her as often as he could until she wished for no more. At the fourth slow penetration Sarah began to writhe almost uncontrollably and by the sixth she was in the midst of a climax of screaming, mind numbing intensity. All the time he was alternating soft kisses with sweet whispers and she was crying out with total abandonment to delight. His penetrations, slowly and meticulously performed, continued long after her climax had subsided and she had opened her eyes and moved her head to look into his face.

"That was amazing," she whispered, and he told her there was more to come.

Almost imperceptibly he increased the speed of his thrusts, supporting himself on one forearm and with each withdrawal inserting his fingers round her clitoris. With her hips high and her head down her vagina was foreshortened and blood flowed to her head, making her feel slightly dizzy as his shaft penetrated her until it struck her womb. With the dextrous fingers doing their work she felt as if she was being slowly stabbed to an intoxicating death, but the feelings changed and she realised that the rigidity of his cock was unabated and that she was stirring again towards her ultimate pleasure. As he pressed forward he began to grind his pubic bone against her clitoris whilst his hand now occupied itself with seeking out the cleft between her buttocks and a long finger worked its way into her anus pulling at her sphincter and making her feel dizzy with delight. He knelt over her and she looked up at the broad shoulders and the powerful chest and she shuddered outward from her cunt to the end of her extremities in a mix of sheer lust and happiness with his sensitive attention to her. Her shudder was accompanied by the opening of her eyes and mouth to their fullest extent and the bucking of her hips against him as he penetrated her again and again until she moaned and howled as her climax hit its peak and she felt his jism strike into her and then spray all over her thighs and belly as he withdrew. She reached up and drew him to her as his throbbing and spurting cock provided a sticky lubricant between them and they kissed as if it was the beginning rather than the end of their passion.

Very gently Mr Expert rose to his knees and then stood up. It was only at that point that Sarah was fully aware of the audience and its applause and she closed her legs and rolled off the cushion. Her partner helped her to her feet and she found herself bowing to the audience and then being turned to leave the stage

The women advanced on Sarah and covered her with the dress which she had worn when she came to the stage. Terry was suddenly at her side urging her to come on.

"But I need to see..."

"No you don't. He is no more real for you than Mr Rough and Mr Brutal. You will only ever meet him once, and that meeting is now over."

Sarah burst into tears of misery at being deprived of this beautiful man who had done everything just as she wanted it and had selflessly given her ultimate pleasure and delight.

"He said he loved me..."

"And very probably at that moment he did, but even more important for your delight was that you should believe it." Sarah's face crumpled and Terry reached an arm round her and held her tight. "Some love lasts almost a lifetime, whilst other love is fierce and brief. Think of this as a wonderful experience with a man who loves with a burning flame, but it is a taper, extinguished by a single breath."

*

The next afternoon and into the early evening they walked in the gardens and grounds of the great house which contained so many surprises and perhaps unrevealed secrets. Their walk was very leisurely because Sarah was still feeling a little frail.

They talked of various things and Sarah felt relaxed enough to eventually confess something to Terry that had been bothering her for some time.

"Since I had this complete change of life I've had curious fantasies about it all connected with the sexual experience," Sarah paused.

"Go on," said Terry.

"It's all to do with sacrificing my life, but in a way which is not for anyone else's good, but is the ultimate in strange events. I have this vague vision of offering myself as a hostage to barbarians or terrorists who, in a society where female nakedness is absolutely taboo, strip me and make me run the gauntlet, naked, whilst they slash at me with whips."

"That sounds a familiar scenario for you."

Sarah looked slightly abashed, but admitted it. "Then they bind me to a St Andrew's cross and abuse me while I hang there with all my limbs spreadeagled."

"Have you tried that with Ivan and Tania?"

"No, only here on my first show and sort of with Mr Expert, but you make me think it might be an interesting idea."

"What happens next?"

"They release me and take it in turns to screw me, two at a time ripping into me at back and front while I submit to their lusts and eventually pass out."

"It all sounds a bit wonderful to me."

"Yes, there's no thought that they may hurt me more than I can stand, nor that they are the disgusting unwashed. There's probably enough there to run a couple of nice acts."

"But do you still want to do such things?"

"Yes, I'm still an exhibitionist and I have a taste for being whipped and I love having an orgasm in public. But something has changed and I don't know whether I want to have encounters with Nick and Ivan anything like as much as I did. I find that of all the things that have happened to me in this training, it's you who's made the difference."

"So, it is the usual sort of performance but with a change of partner? That sort of change has to be very carefully managed. After all, the one you desire most may not be available and you should try out with another woman to see if it is women who now take over with you, or just one woman."

"I don't suppose," said Sarah, "that one's partner in such affairs has to be someone who is a lover."

"I've no idea," Terry admitted, "but we can try to find out. How about if I get a little audience together and we see if you are happy with a woman you don't know?"

"It sounds all right to me, but I wouldn't want to do it if you weren't there."

"I'll be there all right," Terry replied.

They went back to the house and found a light meal awaiting them in Sarah's room. Sarah tried to cajole Terry into staying the night, but she excused herself on the grounds of having to set up the following day's events and kissed Sarah and left.

The next day was routine and when tea time came it was celebrated with a tiny Cornish pasty and some delicate salad and a very small cup of white tea. Just enough, she thought, to keep her blood sugar level up and not enough to get in the way of her performance.

The time seemed to pass very slowly, until there was a knock on the door and Terry stood there wearing what appeared to be a Greek chiton. Whatever it was, it certainly suited her slender, shapely figure. Sarah had had a shower and was still wearing her dressing gown. "What shall I wear?" Sarah asked.

"Come as you are. We have more than half an hour to get you ready."

The walk to the venue was much longer than to the gym and Sarah worked out that they must have left the wing of the house in which she lived and were in the main part of the mansion. They entered a small room equipped with mirrors, lights and chairs and Terry rang a bell. Two women in white jump suits and aprons came in.

"This is Sylvie," Terry told them. "We've discussed what you are to do. You have twenty five minutes. I shall come back at five to eight for her."

The women nodded, pulled out drawers and took all the paraphernalia of makeup artists from them. One gestured to Sarah to stand up and the other removed her dressing gown. Sarah pointed out that she could readily have done it for herself and looked for an answer. The taller of the two women looked hard at her, pointed at her mouth and then shook her head. Sarah realised that her attendants were dumb. She followed their gestured instructions as they worked on her hair, face, body and feet. Whatever their difficulties in life, their hands conveyed the message of super efficiency and competence. A few moments before Terry was due to return they unveiled a full length mirror and invited Sarah to look at herself. She gasped. A naked woman is unlikely to be glamorous, because she is wholly real, but she realised that the two women had achieved the impossible.

Terry entered carrying a tiny bra which was fastened over Sarah's breasts hiding only her nipples, and a G string of equally minute proportions which hardly hid her cleft from view. Terry produced a black silk kimono which was closed at the front with a strip of Velcro. As Sarah moved it clung to every curve of her body and gave tantalising glimpses of wonderfully enhanced skin. She made a half twirl before the mirror and even she was excited by what she saw, the more so because her blonde hair contrasted so well with the embroidered black.

Terry thanked the women and so did Sarah. Without a word Terry led her across the corridor and into a large room in which there was a sort of boxing ring at floor level with chairs on three sides. About twenty people were present occupying easy chairs and sofas with small tables between them carrying quantities of drink.

Terry opened the top and middle ropes of the ring and ushered Sarah in. There was a ripple of applause.

Terry was followed by Maria, who was followed by the other party to the forthcoming show. She entered the ring and went to the other side from Sarah. Terry began to address the audience.

"Ladies and gentlemen. I introduce you again tonight to Sylvie and Carmel, who is appearing here for the first time. I think of this as an essay in black and white, with Sylvie wearing the black kimono in contrast to her hair and skin and Carmel wearing the white kimono in contrast to hers. Neither of the contestants has been rehearsed for this show so I will tell you, and them, that I am the referee, and that what I say goes. Furthermore, in case anyone gets the wrong idea there are three very large gentlemen at the back who will obey me. And only me.

"This will be a contest in totally free style apart from biting and scratching. There will be no rounds, you will both continue until one of you is beaten or submits. I have weighed both contestants and Sylvie is one hundred and fourteen pounds. Carmel is sixteen pounds heavier. However, this contest does not depend on sheer size. At the end, the loser, if she is in a reasonable condition, will receive a good thrashing with a birch, given by the winner, or she may sell her privilege to anyone who makes her an acceptable offer.

"If I say Stop, you break, go to your corner and wait for me to restart the fight."

Sarah wondered what she had let herself in for. Carmel was a bigger woman and appeared to be light on her feet. If she lay on her, Sarah would have difficulty getting out from under her. She remembered all the wrestling she had seen on television and hoped that her karate sessions would prove useful.

Terry stepped up to the centre of the ring and called Sarah and Carmel to her. "We want a good, dirty fight, no running away, but continuous action up to the end. About twenty minutes will please everyone." She stepped back as the two women eyed each other, and shouted "Start!"

Sarah thought that she should try to get the advantage of an immediate strike and launched herself inside Carmel's guard and started punching her in the midriff. Carmel brought down a fair sized fist which Sarah moved away from, but which scraped down the side of her face and hit her shoulder. Sarah stepped back and caught Carmel a sharp blow to the side of her head. So far Sarah's speed had kept her out of trouble and she feinted with her left hand and brought her right fist round and hit Carmel in the ribs. Carmel chopped at Sarah who danced away, but was pursued by Carmel. Neither woman had much idea of ring craft but Carmel managed to back Sarah into a corner. Before she was overwhelmed by the bigger woman Sarah started to rain blows on Carmel's upper body. Carmel ignored them and tried to crush Sarah against the corner post. Sarah raised her left knee to fend off the heavier body, only to find that Carmel had seized her leg and pulled it up, throwing her to the floor and following up her advantage by dropping herself on top of Sarah. She saw her coming and rolled to one side. Most of Carmel missed Sarah, but as She tried to wriggle away Carmel made a grab for her and in the process ripped open Sarah's kimono. She was seriously impeded by the open garment, and rolled away on to her knees and quickly shrugged out of the wide sleeves. This move was met with a round of applause. Carmel approached with her arms raised ready to grasp her in a bear hug, but Sarah stepped to one side and caught one of Carmel's arms in both her hands and twisted her off balance. As she staggered Sarah pulled her arm behind her and forced her to her knees. Carmel was a great deal faster than Sarah had given her credit for and she reached behind her, caught Sarah's hair and as Sarah bent forward she threw her over her shoulder. As she landed in a heap, Sarah realised that she had clutched Carmel's kimono in her flight and had opened it and pulled it up on Carmel's body. Carmel did a reverse somersault out of Sarah's way and was trying to free herself from the garment when Sarah hit her from behind, knocking her over, but receiving a hard kick to the shin for her pains. She ignored the pain and bent and seized Carmel in a headlock. Carmel used her considerable strengthen to try to dislodge Sarah, but with Carmel lying face up and having caught her left arm in the folds of the kimono, Sarah had every advantage and was pressing it home with a steadily tightening grip on Carmel's head.

Carmel, disadvantaged as she was, had decided not to put up with this indignity and flung up both legs, catching Sarah's neck in her feet and ankles. Sarah knew that if Carmel could cross her legs then it would be all over for her, so she released Carmel's head and jumped backwards from a virtual sitting position. Carmel brought her legs down to the ground and attempted to get up, but Sarah was astride her back in an instant and was pulling Carmel's free hand backwards up her back.

This was looking good for Sarah, but Carmel managed to free her trapped arm and reached backwards to Sarah, catching an arm and by main force dragging it away from her own. With only one arm available Sarah wasn't a match for Carmel's sheer strength and Carmel steadily pulled her folded arm down her body. By the time it was nearly parallel with her side, Carmel had started to turn and threw Sarah off her back. She landed untidily and Carmel danced to her feet as Sarah scrambled up. But now Carmel had discarded her kimono and was weighing up Sarah who was amazed at the black woman's body which had very large breasts and a narrow waist which flowed out into wide and powerful hips and thighs. Had it not been for the depression of the bra strap across her breasts, Sarah would have thought Carmel was naked, because the material was virtually the same colour as her skin.

Carmel raised her arms above her head and flexed her muscles to the appreciation of the audience. Sarah launched herself at her waist but found her head buried between Carmel's breasts. Carmel promptly grasped Sarah's head and held it tight against her, almost completely cutting off Sarah's air supply. She flailed at Carmel punching and clawing in desperation. She tried kicking Carmel but the angle of her body and the distance made this virtually impossible. By chance she managed to get hold of Carmel's bra strap and pulled with all her strength. Inevitably it broke and Sarah reached up and took hold of the nipple and a good deal of Carmel's right breast. She sank her fingers into the firm, slightly slippery flesh and clawed Carmel for all she was worth. Carmel let out a howl which was repeated as the same treatment was given to her left breast. Carmel knew she had to get rid of Sarah, or disable her, and she let go of her head and slipped her hand and forearm between Sarah's legs and heaved.

Sarah came off the floor as if she were a doll and let go of Carmel in order to steady herself. Carmel held her off the floor with one arm whilst with the other she tore at Sarah's bra using all her strength. Sarah kicked Carmel for all she was worth, but could find no vital spot. Carmel reached up with her free hand and tried to grasp Sarah's breast, apparently keen to return the agony which she had recently experienced. Sarah grasped the wrist with both hands and began to twist it. Carmel didn't give way easily and Sarah felt her arm between her thighs flex. In a moment Carmel had seized Sarah's G string and had used her strength and weight to dislodge Sarah so that she fell backwards. Carmel was holding Sarah above the ground by her G string cord. The string was cutting her painfully in the crotch and she found that all her shaking and attempted grabbing of Carmel was doing no good. She gave a convulsive leap against Carmel's hands and the G string gave up the unequal struggle and Sarah fell face down, rapidly scrabbling away and not hearing the applause which greeted her nakedness.

Carmel was on her at once and was unlucky that Sarah had moved so fast. She grabbed at the falling Carmel and it was her turn to hold the G string. Either Carmel's weight and velocity or a weaker cord meant that she was left with the G string in her hand. Carmel turned in a flash and knocked Sarah to the floor. She at once sat astride Sarah's chest and leaned down to grasp an arm in each hand. Sarah arched her back giving the audience an excellent view of her thighs and crotch under tension. She couldn't throw Carmel off, but Carmel slid further up Sarah's body until she could use her knees to hold Sarah's arms down.

Carmel seized a breast in each hand and started to knead it. Far from being agonising Sarah recognised this as an agreeable sensation. After a short while Carmel stopped working Sarah's breasts and got her hand round one of Sarah's arms. With a careful manoeuvring she managed to reverse herself on Sarah so that she was now kneeling on Sarah's arms but facing her feet, Sarah tried to lift her legs to catch Carmel in a headlock with her feet. A strong hand pressed against her belly and rendered her efforts quite useless. Carmel had one hand on Sarah's breast and the other seemed to be making its way towards her feet. Carmel opened Sarah's vulva with her thumb and forefinger and inserted three fingers between them. The pressure was perfect and Carmel rubbed Sarah's clitoris, occasionally moving her hand so that the audience, who had crowded to the ropes could see exactly how Sarah was fashioned and just what Carmel was doing to her.

Sarah looked up, but all she could see was Carmel's gaping crotch being lowered on to her face. Sarah heard her say "Lick", and submissively, she did just that. Carmel lowered herself to cover Sarah's mouth and then released one of her arms and said, "Fingers." She released the other and said "Nipples." Sarah inserted her tongue and fingers into Carmel's now very wet and salty tasting vagina whilst her fingers worked on Carmel's erect clitoris and dragged as well as she could at Carmel's nipples and breasts.

Despite her other activities, Sarah's principal concern was for what was happening between her legs. She felt her coming orgasm and tried to avoid it. Her fingers and tongue worked harder and faster on Carmel and she felt her juices begin to drip increasingly rapidly from between her legs. She felt Carmel tense and throw back her head in a howl as she came and then Sarah knew she could have her pleasure and did.

Carmel slowly subsided on top of her and then rolled off and lay at her side with her head on Sarah's belly.

Terry stepped to the centre of the ring as the two women began to come round. "Now, ladies and gentlemen, I think you will agree that that was as good a show as we have seen here and I think we should allow you to choose the winner of this combat. Let's have a vote. Please put your hand up if you want Carmel declared the winner." Terry quickly counted the hands. "And now a vote for Sylvie." There were fewer raised hands.

Terry handed the bundle of birch twigs to Carmel. Before she had a chance to say anything else Carmel had turned to the audience.

"I am prepared to sell my right to thrash Sylvie to the highest bidder. Let me hear a bid for each stroke."

"Fifty pence!" was offered at once, to the amusement of the audience.

"Two pounds."

"Three."

The bidding went on until it reached twelve pounds and it stopped. Carmel was about to hand over the birch when she stopped.

"I can see another birch there. Would anyone like to bid to birch me?"

There was an immediate succession of bids but ten pounds was the highest.

"I see," Carmel said, "just one big spender. Well, I'll tell you what, subject to Terry's agreement, we'll be punished together. How do you arrange these things, Terry?"

"You stand facing the audience and hang your arms over the top rope of the ring, grasping the middle rope. The punisher goes at you until that side is well done. On command you go across to the other side of the ring and stand with your back to the ropes reaching over the top rope as far as you can. The front is then dealt with. The birch twigs are quite brittle so that there will be a limit to the number of strikes, but the victim has no appeal against the strength or target of each blow. The bircher can go on until enough money has been spent or until the twigs break up and are no longer effective."

Sarah stood at her corner of the ring with her arms clasped in front of her. Carmel beckoned to the two winners of the auction who ducked between the ropes and took the proffered birches. The man had removed his jacket and had undone his collar, his tight fitting dove grey trousers revealed a substantial lump at the crotch. The woman was wearing a sleeveless cross over blouse cut very low at the front and tied at the waist with a large bow. Carmel had drawn the man.

The two victims took up their positions hanging over the ropes. Although much more solidly built, Carmel was only fractionally taller than Sarah. To avoid pushing out their bottoms, both of them had had to spread their legs to maintain an almost vertical position.

Sarah was very concerned that although this was much like the whippings she had received before it was different because she had no idea how ruthless the punishment might be or how much damage the birch might do. Carmel's solidly muscular body looked as if it might absorb any punishment that it received, but despite this Sarah realised that Carmel was shivering and sweating in anticipation of the pain she would have to endure. Sarah had already worked out that heavy blows would quickly destroy the birch, but a series of lighter cuts with the sharp springy ends of the birch would mean that there were far more of them and that they would hurt and probably damage just as much.

Terry took command.

"I have this block and hammer here. I shall strike it each time a blow is to be landed and I shall count how many there are. Are you all ready?"

The two victims nodded miserably, though each of them knew that their pain was going to enrich Carmel substantially.

Sarah heard a hollow knock and felt the blinding pain of a dozen sharp cuts into her skin. She gasped and heard Carmel scream and saw her shake. The blows were excruciatingly painful and Sarah groaned as they fell. No rescuing endorphins had yet kicked in and she could feel her back as a mass of very slowly dissipating weals. She felt something slowly trickle down her back and looked down to see that bits of twig had fallen around her. She heard Terry's relentless count and her assailant's devastating attack continued. Sarah gasped and cried out, but Carmel let out an almost continuous howl, swaying her hips and picking her feet up in agony. Each time she did so the following cut was even more powerful and Sarah suddenly realised that she was being showered with a mixture of broken twigs, and Carmel's sweat..

Terry called a halt and ordered the two victims to prepare for their fronts to be dealt with. Both women unhitched themselves from the ropes with some difficulty, staggering as they let go of the supporting rope. Sarah looked at Carmel's glistening black skin, but could not see any wounds from which blood might be issuing. Lots of very small incisions, she thought, and wondered if her tormentor had done equal damage to her. She hooked her arms over the top rope facing the audience, but Terry didn't appear to be happy with either of them and pulled them so that their arms were caught behind their backs and the rope was firmly under their armpits. Having got both women to thrust out their breasts, she pulled their legs forward and apart so that they were leaning back against the rope and unless they moved their feet, were incapable of moving off the rope.

Sarah realised that the woman who was thrashing her was left handed and both tormentors stood at the side of their victim so that every cut was immediately visible to the audience. Both of the executioners had removed their upper garments and Sarah was immediately impressed by the slender figure beside her and her tiny, but tip tilted breasts. Sarah realised that under other circumstances she would have loved to have taken this elegant creature in her arms. As it was she felt totally in her power. The woman leaned towards her and increased her sense of submission by whispering in her ear. "I'm going to flay you alive, and when I've finished with you they will rub you all over with salt. I want to hear you scream now and be beyond screaming then."

Sarah trembled and looked out over the audience who were craning forward, eager to see every bit of the action.

The audience looked their fill at the two naked bodies and then Terry told them she would go on counting. It was worse this time because Sarah could see the birch in the woman's hand and watch her raise it above her shoulder. She tried moving to deflect the coming blow, but realised that she was stuck in a position of total submission and openness. The birch whistled down on her unprotected belly and lightning sprang up from the pain of the blow and engulfed her senses with searing agony. It was followed by another which caught her across the tops of her thighs. She could hear Carmel screaming beside her and as she looked at her companion the third stroke cut her across the breasts with breath taking pain. And yet Sarah realised that what should have been the most dreadful cut so far was not as painful as the earlier ones. She rejoiced in the power of her submissiveness and thrust her pelvis forward. The next cut caught her across the lower part of her belly and spread itself into her crotch. It stung like a crowd of wasps, but she knew that she had gone through the pain barrier and that there might be something to enjoy. Another two slashes saw her receive blows just below her breasts and across them. She felt sweat trickle down her front, but looking down saw that she had been cut and that a tiny rivulet of blood was oozing down her front towards her navel.

She had given up on wondering if the damage that was being done to her was permanent or would be no more than a quickly healing scratch. She was getting to the stage when she was giving herself up to the terrible pleasure of being dominated and being abused. All her latent masochism had swept to the surface. What more could she want than to be exposed, naked, to admiring eyes and to be overwhelmed with pain by a ritual thrashing?

The next blow was just above her knees and was followed by a slash which came up off the floor, scraped the insides of her thighs and landed on her vulva. Sarah let out a howl, but it was different from the screams of her companion. Sarah knew herself well enough now to know that such seemingly totally and blindingly painful cuts at this point were the precursors of her own extreme pleasure. She curved her body back and opened her legs as far as they would go. The bare breasted persecutor struck hard, twice and Sarah began to dissolve. Juice dripped from her and mingled with the tiny splashes of blood that the birch had spread over her. Her hips seemed to take on a life of their own and thrust forward her pelvis and opened her vulva. A final slash should have put a stop to all her delight, but it caught her most sensitive parts and sent her into a paroxysm of delight, evidenced by her lolling head and pouring juices.

As Sarah enjoyed the wonderful sensation of her orgasm, the man who had been thrashing Carmel held up the broken twigs of his birch. Terry called a halt and the woman who had inflicted such agony on Sarah threw hers down and slipped her arm round Sarah's shoulders helping her off the rope and holding her close to prevent her from falling. Sarah's joints responded to the help and she put her arms round the woman's neck and they stood quite still for a long moment until Sarah put her lips to the stranger's mouth and kissed her. The response was to be held even tighter and for the woman's free hand to caress Sarah from breast to clitoris.

Carmel was not so lucky. The man drew his hand across her body and held it up to show the audience the blood which had seeped from dozens of tiny cuts. Without moving her he gripped Carmel's breasts and then slid almost the whole of his hand between her legs, pressing her clitoris with his knuckle. Carmel found this invasion as painful as the beating, but undeterred the man worked furiously at her and she eventually responded to the applause of the audience. Sarah and the woman caressed each other, but Sarah's attempts to do more than cup a tiny breast and roll the nipple between her thumb and forefinger were quite in vain.

Terry was addressing the audience again.

"Well, ladies and gentlemen, I think that was close to the ultimate. All we need now is a round of applause for the three ladies and the gentleman and the handing over of two signed bearer cheques which I will complete and give to Carmel."

Carmel's apparently indifferent partner carefully peeled her from the top rope, and producing a large white handkerchief, carefully blotted her face and began to wipe her body. She reached an arm round his shoulders and he leaned towards her and kissed her with his hand behind her head.

Terry had clearly had enough of all these endearments and called for the protagonists to leave the ring, which they all did, two of them with some difficulty. Terry led them to the changing rooms where there were assistants who took Carmel and Sarah into lukewarm showers and very carefully soaped them with delicate disinfectant and astringent liquid soap, brought them out and wrapped them in large towels, drying every bit of them. They gave the two women and their partners a cup of coffee each, Sarah's and Carmel's had more in it than just milk and coffee and they began to revive. The partners sent for a change of clothing, but remained in the changing room. The two assistants unwrapped each of the women and carefully treated their skin with soothing creams. Unlike what happened with the whips, Sarah could detect no bruises. The cuts were very small, but also numerous and she supposed the same was true of Carmel.

The conversation was desultory as the women were worked on. After a while they were ready to be clothed, and silk dresses were forthcoming. The partners had changed and it was time for them to go. Carmel was gently kissed and her partner left. Sarah was held in a soft embrace by the stranger who whispered in her ear that she thought she was beautiful, and Sarah felt a small piece of card pressed into her hand.

Terry ushered the assistants and the two partners out, and, having spoken to the latter in the corridor returned and handed Carmel two slips of paper.

"These are yours, Carmel, and no one can say you didn't earn them."

Carmel looked at the cheques and gaped. "It was almost worth it," she said.

Sarah smiled at her and told her that they would make a wonderful double act.

"I'd go for that," Carmel told her, "and here's your first pay cheque." She handed Sarah a cheque which Sarah tried to refuse. "You see," she told Carmel, I enjoyed it all in a funny sort of way."

"So did I, but most of all our contact."

"I liked that, but I liked being beaten, too."

"No accounting for tastes," Carmel replied and they parted.

What Sarah most wanted was to go to her room, curl up in bed and have something to eat. She remembered the card in her hand and saw it had a name and address on it with a note on the back 'Hope we can meet.'. She felt a sudden skip of her heart and wondered if she might meet this woman again and what would happen.

Terry broke in on this reflection, coming through the door without her usual knocking.

"Are you all right?" Terry asked.

"It depends what you mean by all right. You know exactly what I've been through because you set it up. Still I suppose someone cares about me."

"You know I do."

"Just for once I wasn't thinking about you." Sarah's tone was very cool and Terry registered uneasiness.

"Then who? Just because Carmel did the decent thing with that cheque doesn't mean..."

"And not Carmel, either," Sarah replied and looked away from Terry.

"You seemed to manage very well with close contact from two women," Terry observed.

"Yes, you have made a difference in me, except it might not be quite the one you were looking for. I'm really turned on by women and I want to explore and find out about more of them, so that I'm not stuck on just one person like I was with Nick and I thought I was with you."

"So, you are now in search of the ideal woman and I suppose you don't want to be an exhibitionist or a masochist any more?"

"I am well aware that the ideal woman probably doesn't exist, if only because I have changed and I'll continue to change and what suited me yesterday will probably not suit me today."

"That just sounds like being very fickle, or promiscuous."

"You can call it what you want, but I don't manipulate people, though I do try to get my own way."

"You seem to be forgetting my part in all this."
"Not at all, I owe you a great deal for opening my eyes to things which I hadn't realised existed. On the other hand that was what you were supposed to do. Today showed me that I've changed far enough."

"Then I think that this training must come to an end."

"Good. I've been frightened, I've been physically, mentally and emotionally hurt, but I've also been very bored. Unless you are going to kill me I rather think that I'd like to go home."

"Very well, I'll go and consult and then make the necessary arrangements."

*

Heidi was tidy and methodical. The flat was polished and hoovered, things were put away where they should be, there was never washing up in the sink. What had to be put in the washer was there when it became dirty and was washed at once and dried and ironed as soon as it was ready. Heidi wrote neat lists to remind herself what was wanted at the local convenience store. She marked up the calendar with their gigs, but used a code which wouldn't leave the reader any the wiser. She kept a diary of events in their lives and of her feelings about them. They went to Tate Modern and she provided a quite elaborate criticism of several of the items. She was an ardent reader and included notes on what she was reading. Each page was ended with a list of things to do the following day.

Nick continued much as before, but he had become used to Heidi and comfortable with her in the home and in his bed. She could be placid, indifferent, inventive or wild depending on how she felt. Nick noticed that she was also becoming somewhat like Sarah in deriving satisfaction from being exhibited and abused. Mostly, in their domestic situation, she was strong and helpful. Nick watched the days pass, carefully marked off on the calendar and wondered what would happen when Sarah finished her training. His thoughts must have touched something in Heidi's consciousness as she turned towards him one day.

"What are we going to do when Sarah comes back?"

"I was just thinking about it," Nick replied.

"Thinking of two for the price of one?"

"Certainly not," Nick told her. "But I do have a responsibility towards you both."

"You didn't invite me here, I came to you, though I must say I reckon it worked out well. But you don't owe me anything."

"You sound as if you would be happy not to have any more."

"I don't think I would be happy, but it's your decision."

"We'll talk it through when she comes back. The trouble is I reckon I feel the same about you as I do about her."

"We'll try and do whatever seems right on the day. She's been away for a month and she'll be changed. I can't tell you how, but she will have changed. We'll just have to listen carefully to whatever she has to say to us."

"OK."

"We've got a fairly routine gig tomorrow night and then four days off. I'll try to find out what's happening to Sarah and when she's likely to be home."

*

Sarah had been given a wad of notes, a brand new outfit complete with a change of clothes and more than one of underwear, and had been driven in a closed car to London and had been dropped off, at her own request, in Curzon Street. She pulled a mobile phone from her brand new handbag and consulted the piece of card tucked behind it in its leather cover. She punched in the number and waited. Two, three, four rings and the phone was picked up. She recognised the voice.

"This is Sylvie," Sarah said, "and I thought I would ring you."

The voice at the other end appeared to be genuinely pleased to hear from her.

"You're right," she went on. "It is soon, but I was let go. Yes I am sore, but everything is fading and healing quickly. Did you mean what you said? Can I come to see you? Now?"

Sarah slung the wide strap of her bag across her shoulders and gripped it in one hand. She set off to walk to the street nearby. She arrived and looked at the entry phone. There were three names, the top one was the one she needed. As the door opened she was amazed to see her tormentor standing in the entrance hall with her arms outstretched.

They ascended in the lift to the top of the house. Laura seemed to occupy the top floor. The apartment was large and beautifully decorated and furnished. Sarah was overcome by the understated evidence of wealth and good taste.

"Put your bag down over there and we'll have a cup of tea."

Laura left her and Sarah gazed out of the window, looking out over Hyde Park. The traffic was at its usual murderous thickness down below, but was completely inaudible owing to the triple glazing. Some sort of air conditioning system provided clean, perfectly balanced and temperature controlled ventilation. Sarah turned away as Laura returned with a tray. They shared a white leather sofa and Laura started to pour out the tea. As she handed Sarah her cup and saucer, Sarah blushed.

"I feel clumsy and yobbish, You don't know me at all and yet I want to ask you a great favour. But I don't think I should." Sarah began to stumble over her words, but Laura turned to her and put two cool fingers on her lips.

"You want to know if you can stay here, is that it?" Laura asked.

"How did you know?" Sarah was aghast.

"It's not that long since we met, but I have to tell you that as a founder member I had the right to know everything that was known about you, and I exercised that right. Then I knew that your training had ended, so that whatever change was wanted for you had been successful. I knew what you were like before the training so I had a fair idea what that change might be. Then you turn up here with a largish bag which appears to contain clothes. Either you've done a very rapid shop, or you have the clothes given at the end of training and you need somewhere to stay."

"Oh, dear. I must seem totally transparent to you. You're quite right, but it was not just a matter of needing somewhere to stay, I wanted to see you again."

"And I wanted to see you, so there is absolutely no harm done and I'm delighted that you want to stay. You need to think before you commit yourself to your next move."

"You're right again."

"Very well. It might be useful to have someone to talk them over with. I'll try to be a sounding board, but I can't promise to be a totally disinterested listener. My interest is you." Laura leant forward and brushed Sarah's cheek with her lips. Sarah felt a little thrill run down her face and neck. This was a good omen, she thought.

"I'll show you round the place after we've had this tea."

The apartment was very large with four bedrooms and as many bathrooms. Each room was equipped with its own climate control and the bedrooms were each decorated and furnished in different pastel shades.

"You may have whichever suits you," Sarah was told. She chose one with a large and beautiful Victorian bed with all the usual brass and wrought iron fittings so beloved of the rich in the nineteenth century. She was instructed in the use of the remote control to open the concealed wardrobe doors, adjust the air conditioning, bring out the television from its hiding place and operate it, complete with the DVD player and CD player.

"I have a library of DVDs and CDs and you're welcome to borrow any you want. I have the bedroom next door. If there's anything you want, just ask. By the way, four people come in every morning at seven thirty and clean the place and tidy up. They are officially blind, deaf and dumb, and very well paid. If you want to walk about naked when they're here they won't see you, though they may admire you.

They'll knock discreetly when they're ready to do your room. If you don't want to be disturbed, just don't answer."

Sarah unpacked her few clothes and found that the bag contained two silk dresses, a pair of jeans and a cropped top which was so cropped it was almost not worth wearing, a silk night-dress and a matching dressing gown. There was four days supply of underwear and two pairs of shoes and a pair of pumps. Her bathroom contained towels, face flannels, various versions of soap and a quantity of lotions and make up.

Sarah wandered back into the drawing room and found Laura with a pile of newspapers beside her.

"I forgot to ask you, which of your names do you prefer to be called by?"

"Sarah, for friends."

"Thank you. By the way, you were cut about rather badly, I have some excellent stuff in a bottle which will quieten everything down."

Sarah went for a shower, wrapped herself in a warm towel and called Laura who appeared with a bottle in her hand.

"You do your front and I'll do your back. Then you should walk about for ten minutes or so to let the lotion dry before putting on your clothes."

Sarah found herself totally at ease with Laura and within half an hour was back in the drawing room sunk deep into the sofa with her feet up on a foot rest and gazing out of the window at the trees and buildings that were within sight.

"Do you think I could stay with you until I straighten out my head about Nick?"

"Of course, and depending on what happens, if you want to continue here I'll be happy to have you. I warn you that you can't just walk away from your training. There will be times and places when we will have to go separately or together and most times you will perform and sometimes I will, and there may be times when we are together."

"I'd like that. Look, they gave me a wad of notes when I left them. You must have at least half as an advance on rent."

"No thanks. I'm not short of money."

"You said that as if there was something else you were short of."

"Yes, but we'll come to that in due course. Tell me, why did you choose to come here. You had the resources to go to a hotel, or you could have gone straight home to Nick."

"You frightened me, and then you treated me exactly as I wished and you are beautiful and elegant and I had no idea who you were or anything about you, but I treasured that little card and I so wanted to see you again."

"And I wanted to see you. I thought you were brave and very sexy and that we might just have enough in common for us to rub along together."

"I do hope so."

"I suggest that in due course I will send out for something to eat-yes, I do cook, but it will be better to have something brought in tonight. Then we could perhaps decide on a strategy for how you are to approach Nick. I'm anxious that you don't hurt his feelings and. I've readied myself to the idea that you may decide here that you would rather be with me, but when you see him you could very easily change your mind."

"I'm anxious about that, too. I suppose the best thing for me to do is to turn up on the doorstep when he comes back from work tomorrow night and talk to him. I haven't had any contact with him for weeks, but then, that was part of the agreement. I was a bit upset at the time that he hadn't insisted on discussing the whole arrangement with me. I didn't like the fact that he was apparently my owner, either."

"What do you mean?"

"Well, I gather they asked him first to see that it was all right by him, and my agreement was very nearly taken for granted."

Their conversation continued until Laura looked at her watch, picked up her phone called a number on the memory and asked what the dishes of the day were. She repeated them to Sarah and asked if any of them appealed. Sarah thought they certainly did and quickly made up her mind. A sweet course was refused. Within a quarter of an hour Laura admitted two immaculately dressed waiters who propelled a large trolley. Within a minute there were flowers on the table, napkins, cutlery, wine glasses, a bottle of something white in an ice bucket and condiments and sauces. They were invited to the table and from a hot cupboard in the trolley their choices appeared and were expertly spooned onto their plates. Sarah had a side salad with French dressing and crisp French bread instead of potatoes. Laura had a selection of vegetables, all perfectly al dente.

Sarah suddenly realised that she was hungry and followed Laura's lead in making a start on what turned out to be a delicious meal, still as hot as when it left the chef's kitchen.

"This is lovely," Sarah remarked.

"It comes from the hotel down the road. We just leave everything on the table and they collect it all when the cleaners come."

"Organised, or what?" Sarah interjected admiringly.

It took them some time to work their way through the meal and to do justice to about three quarters of the bottle of wine.

"You've been up a long time," Laura remarked, and we're going to the gym and then shopping tomorrow and we'll walk to the shops, if not back from them. If you fancy an early night I think I could do with one too, but we'll need to re-anoint you first."

"That's very kind of you, it seems to be working."

"I'm going to have a bath, so we'll meet in your room in, say, half an hour."

Sarah had never seen an automatic temperature regulator on a bath tap before, but she dialled in 103 degrees F and as she finished the outlet was sealed and water gushed into the bath. She stepped out of her clothes and proceeded to brush her teeth. She tried to keep an eye on the water level, but she needn't have bothered because the tap turned itself off when there was about twenty five centimetres of water in the bath. She had added some agreeable bath essence and she slid into the welcoming warm water, thinking she'd have it just a little warmer next time.

When she stepped out of the bath she realised that running it had activated the towel rails. Her bath towel was soft, slightly rough to the touch and warm.

Laura was waiting for her with her lotion bottle in her hand. She was dressed in a chiffon negligee and had her hair tied up at the nape of her neck.

"Let's have a look at you, then."

Sarah stood still as Laura inspected her front and back. "Just a couple which look a tiny bit angry, but we can deal with those tonight and they will be close to gone in the morning. The rest are fading fast."

Laura carefully spread the lotion over Sarah's body and the slightly astringent, but undoubtedly soothing liquid worked its way into her skin.

"I think that's the lot," Laura announced. "Now you can walk about until it dries."

Sarah did as she was told and was surprised to find that Laura had turned down the bedspread and had pulled back the duvet on both sides and had stepped into the bed, leaning against the pillows and bed head.

"Do you mind?" she asked. It was not a question that could possibly be answered by 'yes', even if Sarah had been so inclined. Sarah brushed her hair as she quietly walked about the room and began to think that ten minutes was a very long time. Eventually she stopped by what she had thought of as her side of the bed and bent over Laura and kissed her first on the cheek and then on the lips. As she broke away she heard Laura whisper, "Can I stay at your place, please?" and entering into the spirit of the request she replied, "I won't hear of anything else."

Laura slid down into the bed and for a moment wriggled to get a comfortable position. Sarah realised that she had managed to get rid of the negligee. Sarah dimmed the lights and turned towards Laura who was lying on her side and slipped one arm under Sarah's neck and drew her towards her with the other. Sarah sighed deeply and Laura pressed her body against Sarah and her lips to Sarah's mouth. Sarah grasped Laura by one buttock and gave it a squeeze. Laura pressed her pubic bone against Sarah's and Sarah could feel Laura's sharp erect nipples against her breasts.

"Nothing too exciting, tonight," Laura suggested and produced two little tubes from under her pillow. "These can be very comforting held in the right place," she told Sarah. "Would you like to come?" Sarah knew that she would. "We'll have one of these each and see which of us comes first. All you do is press the end, once for gentle, once more for fierce and again for off." She kissed Sarah and moved her thighs to open her sex. Sarah did the same and both of them pressed the little magic tubes between their thighs. Sarah started off gently and managed to get the three tiny shining knobs on the end of the tube straight on to her clitoris. The effect was sensational. Her hand began to buzz and her clitoris seemed to absorb the sensations which the machine produced and flood them out across her belly. After a very short time, or so it seemed to Sarah, she began to crave even more and pressed the end again. This time the effect was quite devastating. Her hand felt almost numb, but her clitoris had caught fire and was so engorged it protruded way beyond the normally covering lips. Meanwhile, Laura had turned to lie on her back with her legs stretched out rigidly before her and her abdomen a mass of tense muscles. She was pressing the tube hard against herself with one hand whilst roughly kneading her breasts with the other.

For Sarah this was a new experience and she had been unprepared for the effects wrought by the inoffensive little tube. She felt her pelvic floor muscles begin to tense and suddenly she was all liquid, spilling over from her crotch and soaking down between her thighs into the bed clothes. As she struggled to press the tube again she realised that she had slipped it inside herself and that it appeared to be contacting her G spot so that her orgasm was developed to immense proportions and seemed to go on for ever. Laura had been slightly longer in attaining her climax, but had howled and spurted and had left the tube to its work for perhaps thirty seconds so that she might enjoy the sensation to its conclusion.

Sarah was being driven crazy by the insistent and tyrannical machine inside her and tried to reach up with her fingers to remove it. It was wet and unbelievably slippery and Sarah found that it was so deep in her that she couldn't get a grip on it. Its work was continuing and Sarah feared that she would have climax after climax until she lost consciousness. She found herself calling to Laura for help.

Laura was all concern and solicitude. "What is it darling? Don't tell me, you've shoved it inside yourself and now you can't get it out!"

Sarah gasped that this was true.

"Don't worry, just relax and slip your feet and legs out of the bed and sit up."

Sarah did as she was told and felt the shortening of her vagina from the change of position force the tube against the inner wall of her vagina at the front. Laura was standing in front of her.

"Stand up, Sarah. Legs apart, raise your arms to vertical and when I say push, do it."

Laura inserted her elegant hand into Sarah's vagina, her fingers searching for the tube. After a moment she got some sort of purchase on it with two fingers and gave it a quick pull. "Push!" she commanded, and her hand and the tube were ejected by the strength of Sarah's well toned muscles. Sarah sank to a sitting position on the bed and whispered her thanks to Laura who merely laughed and told her that when the tube had run its battery down, a bit of gentle cold water treatment would have made the entire area less engorged and it probably would have fallen out of its own accord.

"Thanks, I'll remember that," Sarah said ruefully, wondering how many orgasms she might have had in half an hour.

"It's my fault, I should have warned you. I had the

same experience and in my case the answer was eleven and almost total exhaustion. Come on, we'll go to my room. Some nice women have made this bed very damp!"

They retreated to Laura's room and fell into a quiet sleep enfolded in each other's arms.

*

Heidi and Nick had gone off to their gig with Ivan and Tania. The two women had performed the dance of the seven veils for their masters and whilst the audience had appreciated the titillating artistry of the dancers, their masters had been less approving. The inevitable result had been that the two women were set on to fight one another whilst the men plied them with whips to encourage their efforts. Each tried every trick to subdue the other, but the careful rehearsal meant that the whole performance continued until Heidi slipped her hand between Tania's legs and tried to lift and throw her. It would have been a good move, except that Tania had become slippery and Heidi missed her grip and found herself with a couple of fingers in Tania's bottom and Tania well off the ground. Tania went rigid and Heidi attempted to remove her fingers whilst they were both slashed by the whips, Tania reached a hand to Heidi's crotch, inserted her fingers in her vagina and squeezed. Heidi howled and began to sink to her knees whilst Tania dripped juices from between her legs and Heidi tried to drop Tania, who had secured an arm lock round Heidi's neck, and not succeeding, pressed her fingers further into Tania in return for the grip that Tania had got on her crotch. Heidi could not cope with the pain that Tania was inflicting and sank to her knees and tried to roll away from her. The audience roared their approval and Tania transferred her free arm to Heidi's breasts and took one in her hand and the other in her mouth, biting the nipple with sharp white teeth. Heidi screamed and let go of Tania and tried to rise, but was unable to get further than her widespread knees. Tania had slipped her hand under Heidi's buttocks and was endeavouring to get the whole of it into Heidi's vagina. Heidi could no longer support herself and tipped over backwards whilst Tania sat on her chest as if she were riding a horse and, kneeling, opened herself and worked busily on her clitoris until Heidi received the stream of juice across her breasts. The whipping had ceased and after a few moments the four of them bowed to the audience whose applause indicated their appreciation. Heidi stood in front of Nick whose erection was pressing into her buttocks. The not unusual cry of "Fuck her!" was taken up by the audience and Nick bent her double, pulled aside the scrap of cloth which was serving, quite ineffectively to cover his manhood and taking his erection in his hand introduced it at the lips of Heidi's sex.

She was more ready for him than he thought she might be and a mixture of her own and Tania's juices lubricated the way. He pressed home and Heidi raised her head. He pulled her up to standing in front of him and ran his hands over the front of her body, dwelling on her clitoris and breasts. Heidi reached her arms above her head and tried to encircle Nick's neck, but failed and made do with reaching behind her, thrusting out her chest and her breasts as a result.

Nick worked savagely on her clitoris and began to feel a drip from her crotch. He bent her to ninety degrees and started to pump in and out of her. At each thrust her mouth opened and a cry escaped her. All too soon Heidi began to buckle at the knees with the onset of another orgasm and Nick slipped both hands around the front of her waist and speared her as hard as he could until he, too, produced an orgasm which prompted him to withdraw and spurt his hot jism over Heidi's back and buttocks as a fitting finale to the act.

They returned home with a sizeable wedge of cash each to invest in untraceable assets.

They had a drink, another shower and tumbled into bed.

Nick had become used to long nights followed by a day's work. He considered it was the quality of the sleep, rather than its length which mattered. In any case he could catch up at the weekend, or even have an early night on the day following. Heidi had never talked to Nick about her other occupation, but she kissed him goodbye in the morning, usually fully dressed for going out. Soon after he left the house in the morning she, too, was gone.

She managed to be back by five most afternoons, and had a cup of tea waiting for him.

This was an attention he very much enjoyed and appreciated. However, that evening was to be different.

Sarah stood in the privet shaded entry of the house next door and waited for Nick to appear. Her timing was good and it was not a long wait. As he reached out his key to unlock the door she silently mounted the steps behind him and as he pushed open the door, she brushed against him and said "Hallo, Nick."

He stood just inside the door as if transfixed. Sarah was about to say something when Heidi walked into the hallway. She was nothing like as overcome as Nick.

"Hallo, you must be Sarah. Don't just stand there, Nick. Would you like a cup of tea? We were just going to have one."

The banality of the greeting and the offer of refreshment cut straight across Sarah's desire to be acid and demanding. Heidi had gone back to the kitchen and Nick had recovered sufficiently from his surprise to usher Sarah into the sitting room.

"How are you? Are you all right? What are you doing here? I thought you would...."

"Look Nick, it strikes me that you've already told me a lot. You might have introduced me to, to..."

"That's Heidi. You've met her before. She has been ensuring that the gigs have continued."

"I see, she's your partner."

"Yes, exactly."

"And she does with you what we used to do?"

"Oh, yes," Nick replied.

"I've been away more than a month, I come back here and you greet me like a schoolmate you hadn't seen for a day or two. Frankly, you just don't seem to be pleased to see me."

"Oh, no. Of course I'm glad to see you. I was just surprised."

"And there's Heidi to account for. I assume she lives here."

"Well, yes. She lived out in the sticks and it was too late to go home and it just seemed to develop from there."

"And how far has it developed, might I ask?" Sarah's tone was grim. Nick looked guilty and confused by turns. Heidi came in carrying a tray with cups and saucers on it.

"Well, we share a bed and we have quite frequent sex and he's getting better at it. I'm not sure if we are lovers, but we both appear to be working at it."

"You see, Sarah....." Nick began, but Sarah wasn't having any.

"Shut up, Nick. I stay away for four weeks, very largely because you thought you could dispose of me. I come back to find I've been supplanted in bed and at work. Do you agree, Heidi?"

"It's up to Nick to make up his own mind about who he lives with and what he does. I can't speak for him."

"That's a pity, I thought I might get some sense out of you and avoid Nick's fumbling about with reality."

"I had to do it, Sarah, just to keep the jobs coming in."

"And that's why you share our home with a stranger?"

"Heidi isn't a stranger," Nick replied, dropping himself even further into the hole he was busy digging.

"Obviously not. I've had a bloody hard time over the last month and I have had no sex with the men who were available, but you seem to have forgotten my existence in about five minutes and have taken up with Heidi. I do hope she's now got some inkling about the sort of man you are and that she won't get hurt like I've been." Sarah's tone was a mix of piety, disappointment and unhappiness. Each was designed to further upset Nick.

"No, it's not like that, Sarah. I knew you'd come back to me, and here you are."

"You're lying, and I reckon Heidi should be bloody furious."

Nick turned to Heidi and attempted to make his peace with her but he was too late.

"So, you're going to throw me out in favour of Sarah?"

Nick showed every sign of wishing that he was anywhere but where he was.

"I think I've had enough of this," Sarah told him. "You might as well make sure that one of us is happy, and it certainly isn't going to be me. Just get hold of some good quality bags and put all my clothes and possessions in them, neatly packed, mind. Leave them by the front door and I'll be round in two days to pick them up. Then there's the small matter of my share of the house. Leave me a note of what you are prepared to pay me, in cash, with the bags. A serious amount, please. Don't try to fob me off with some paltry sum. I will let you know what I think of your offer and I just hope we can agree without bringing in the lawyers. Right, that's a funny homecoming and not the one I wanted but I trust you will be happy and prosper together."

"I don't know about together," Heidi said quietly as Sarah let herself out of the front door and walked down the road. She half expected Nick to come running after her, but she was not at all disappointed that he didn't. She turned into the next road and saw Laura's Aston Martin at the kerb. She stepped in and Laura turned to her and raised an eyebrow.

"Curiously, very much what you had prepared me for. There was a very attractive woman called Heidi who is apparently another performer, and they've been performing in public and private ever since I left. Nick's in a frantic state and I think may just have said enough wrong things for Heidi to go back to her own place. I told him to pack my clothes and belongings and then make me an offer for my part of the house. I have to come back in two days to collect my stuff and receive the offer."

"You didn't give him an address?"

"Certainly not, but I think I'm imposing on you."

"Then you didn't enjoy last night or this morning?"

Sarah kissed her. "You know I did and if you're prepared to have me in your house I'll work hard to make it even better, if that's possible."

"Oh, yes, that's entirely possible."

Anna is one of the most unforgettable of Silver Moon heroines. From the moment she reports for work at Sinclair Precision Components; pure, innocent and trusting her employers recognise that she has hidden depths and set about bringing them to light. She rapidly finds herself in the hands of a centuries old slave dealing concern and is ruthlessly trained for a life of sexual servitude.

Giselle Lorimer's first book for Silver Moon vividly traces the progression of the sweet natured Anna from innocence to total subjugation with a concentrated eroticism we have seldom published before. Giselle brings her own understanding of female submissiveness to bear with devastating effect and the final acts of submission rank very high in Silver Moon's firmament.

The grim chateau of Beaucastel casts its shadow over the lives of all the slaves who enter its portals. In its cellars and dungeons they undergo training which will forever bind them to their masters and mistresses. But for Verena and Marina, it holds a very different destiny. When they pass through the doors of Beaucastel, nothing will ever be the same for them again.

Caroline Swift writes with an intimate knowledge of the lives of wealthy and cosmopolitan dominants, and draws the reader into a world that is unforgettably erotic. Beaucastel will take its rightful place as a classic of its kind.

Kim Knight's Mia is left at the scene of a minor car crash by the driver. A police car arrives but her troubles are very far from being over.

A woman awakes to find herself in the hands of a satanic cult in Richard Garwood's tale.

Syra Bond's story of a strange meeting on a hot night in New Orleans is hauntingly erotic.

Sean O'Kane's story, simply entitled 'Slave' will stay in the reader's mind for a long time.

Caroline Swift contributes a 'lost' incident from her novel 'The Sufferers'.

Falconer Bridges gives us a teasing glimpse into his forthcoming novel.

William Avon contributes a characteristically sharp account of a woman in captivity.

Silver Moon's authors dish up another feast of piquantly erotic fiction such as only they can devise!

There are over 100 stunningly erotic novels of domination and submission in the Silver Moon catalogue. You can see the full range, including Club and Illustrated editions by writing to:

> Silver Moon Reader Services
> Shadowline Publishing Ltd,
> No 2 Granary House
> Ropery Road,
> Gainsborough,
> Lincs. DH21 2NS

You will receive a copy of the latest issue of the Readers' Club magazine, with articles, features, reviews, adverts and news plus a full list of our publications and an order form.